Return to Paradise

by

A. Arbour

Chapbook Press

Schuler Books
2660 28th Street SE
Grand Rapids, MI 49512
(616) 942-7330
www.schulerbooks.com

Return to Paradise

ISBN 13: 9781966196167

eBook ISBN: 9781966196174

Library of Congress Control Number: 2025902213

Printed in the United States.

FOREWORD
Roger J. Crum

This is a work of fiction, yet its story is about a real place—the lighthouse at Whitefish Point—; a core set of actual people—Bertha ("Bertie") Endress Rollo, her grandparents Robert and Anna Carlson, and her brother Robert "Bobbie" Endress—; and a "supporting cast," even "antagonists" as it were of other verifiable individuals—the Reverend William Law and Mr. and Mrs. Schroeder. Principally the story concerns the years Bertie and her family lived lives of relative isolation at Whitefish Point, a separate existence interrupted only by their occasional, pleasant visits with Reverend Law, and their co-existence of a very different nature with the Schroeders.

By definition, then, this is historical fiction, most notably because it is supported and carried forward by a set of key archival documents that are either quoted in full or used throughout the novel without modification or embellishment: these include Robert Carlson's letter to the Lighthouse Inspector, his "Keeper's Oath of Office," the letter from the Treasury Department appointing Anna Carlson to the position of Assistant Lighthouse Keeper at the Marquette Lighthouse, Bertha Endress Rollo's memoir of her childhood lived at Whitefish Point, and her obituary. Unless indicated otherwise, all other characters, places, and incidents are products of authorial license born of imagination in the service of weaving together the often-disconnected surviving facts of history into a coherent, even dramatic narrative, but not a narrative so dramatic as to be untrue.

*"There is nothing more frightening or exciting
than a blank piece of paper.
Frightening because you're on your own,
leaving dark tracks across that snowy plain,
and exciting because no one knows
your destination but yourself,
and even you can't say exactly where you'll end up."*

—author Robert R. McCammon

RETURN TO PARADISE
SEPTEMBER 13, 1996

Bertie was late for the 10 a.m. tour at the Whitefish Point Lighthouse. She had left plenty of time that September morning to drive west from Sault St. Marie to Paradise, tracing the southern shore of the big lake on the Lake Superior Shoreline Drive. But, as so often happened, her eyes were not exactly fixed on the sparsely traveled spiderweb-veined tar-patched road with the variegated greens of the northern forest to her left and the deepest darkest navy blue lake on her right. Instead, her eyes flicked from side-to-side scanning for birds—all of which she could identify on the wing. Inevitably, a birding detour caused Bertie to pull off onto the shoulder and come to a stop.

She quickly reached into the glove box to retrieve her binoculars to observe the much busier avian traffic winging its way above the road. Focusing the binoculars, she confirmed from the silhouette and flight pattern that she was seeing a flock of black terns crossing her path. She had suspected black terns because of their characteristic swooping and diving acrobatics. While watching the scene on her windshield-wide stage, Bertie held her breath in awe.

She put on her headscarf to protect her hairdo for tomorrow's "big do" and got out of the car. She didn't give a second thought as to whether she should navigate the uneven terrain to the lakeshore. The octogenarian credited her spryness to decades of birding and botanizing.

She picked her way through the fringe of trees—like eyelashes barely obscuring the view of the lake—and spent several minutes training her binoculars on the shorebirds. She spotted the familiar killdeers. These she regarded, like so many of the species of birds she studied, as her fly-by-night companions. They, too, returned to The Point year after year.

What she saw next she'd seen many times before. A mother killdeer feinting a broken wing. As if on cue, a mother killdeer pretended to have a broken wing to lure a predator. This time the predator was a sizeable seagull, being lured away from the killdeer nest of mottled eggs in their stick creche on the rain-dimpled sand. Bertie had learned at a young age about predator-prey relationships in nature. Nevertheless, she pondered that it was much easier for humans to accept this "law of nature" but not that they themselves regularly threaten the lives of others. It was no wonder that on this morning of all mornings she was thinking on this as she drove closer and closer to a quiet place that not only seemed like paradise but was named Paradise.

As Bertie resumed her drive to Whitefish Point, she imagined the birds on their migratory flyway heading to The Point ahead of her. Their bird's eye view of the light station would lend itself to human-watching: birders, rock collectors, ship watchers, and tourists milling about and entering half a dozen white buildings clustered around the lighthouse tower and intermittently looking up to study the lighthouse tower. Bertie mused that the birds could look down and see all that, but they could not know, as she did, that the roof of the lighthouse keepers' residence concealed a house divided underneath.

Bertie soon passed the first of the road signs that signaled she was near home: Paradise. She whispered the destination's name on the breath of a nostalgic sigh.

Because she had lost track of time while bird watching, she was late to return home (this time for the first morning tour) like so many times in her childhood. As she parked, she noted that no one would be there to chastise her, like her grandmother had done many times. Just as she was getting out of her car, a sudden downpour sent pellets of rain that needled her headscarf, turning her head into a pincushion and chasing her past the percussion of the rain on the parked cars, indoors to the shelter of the nearest building—the museum gift shop.

This was a strange "homecoming." On this occasion, she would stay at the lighthouse station crews' quarters, not the lighthouse where she had grown up. And tomorrow, her childhood home would be dedicated to her. That was nice, but she thought it should be dedicated to her grandparents, Robert and Anna Carlson, who raised her at the light. The Carlsons were the longest-serving lighthouse-keeping family at Whitefish Point. They had been stationed together at several lighthouses before being posted to The Point. Given that

Bertie's grandmother was a full partner in the enterprise (with or without the official title of assistant lighthouse keeper), her grandfather wasn't inclined to "pull rank" very often in their work or relationship. Between the job of the keeper and the assistant keeper, there hadn't been much of a difference in rank. Both keepers climbed the same number of steps and made the same number of trips to the lantern room each day.

Anna Carlson certainly had proven her mettle over the years—not the least when her husband left her alone for several days at the Michigan Island lighthouse with their twin infant sons and toddler daughter when a fishing trip turned into a mishap. Many decades later, Anna was hailed as "The Heroine of Michigan Island" in an article published by the National Park Service.

Still, it was to be Bertie, and not her grandparents, who would be honored at the dedication ceremony the next day. She was truly surprised when she found out that the Great Lakes Shipwreck Historical Society had made this decision. When she shared this news with her brother Bobbie over the phone a few months earlier, he, too, was surprised.

"What did you do? Give 'em a bunch of money?" Bobbie asked.

"Well, if you must know, it wasn't a bunch, but I did make a bequest of some size to the Shipwreck Museum in my will, and of course I did just publish my memoir of our life there at the light," Bertie answered defensively.

"Well, that explains everything," Bobbie said flatly.

"That doesn't 'explain everything.' I contributed my memories, and my advice was sought out numerous times by the Historical Society. I also contributed many items from our grandparents' things," Bertie explained. She had relinquished these items a bit sooner than she could easily part with them. Yet, she looked forward to seeing their placement when she toured the house museum.

"It's good you were able to find a place for some of that old stuff," Bobbie said sighing.

"That 'stuff' has historical significance," Bertie countered.

"You're more sentimental, more the historian I should say, than I am about such things," Bobbie conceded. Then he leaned in as if Bertie were seated across from him, dropped his voice, and ventured a personal question. "So, just how much did you give?" Bobbie pressed.

"Let's just say I pledged enough to fund their education outreach program," Bertie said proudly.

If she had one real regret in her life, it was that she never got to finish her college degree at the University of Michigan. She liked to think that she might have gotten a degree in education and had a teaching career. Giving money to the lighthouse station would help to ensure that many students would visit Whitefish Point and be inspired to learn about the history and significance of lighthouse keeping. In this way, she would get to be a teacher after all. Because of this, she was quite eager to attend the dedication ceremony. So, Bertie had decided to arrive a day early for the dedication—before she would be the center of attention—

to spend some time on her own contemplating the truly significant contributions of both her grandparents and what it continued to mean that she and Bobbie had grown up in that extraordinary place.

As it turned out, even with her stop to do some birding, she still was a bit early for the next tour. This gave her time to browse the crowded gift shop. As Bertie navigated around the other customers, she noticed what interested them—playing cards, mugs and shot glasses, keychains and magnets, t-shirts and sweatshirts, etc. Nothing was of particular interest to her, except, of course, her memoir book *Beneath the Light*. A small bookshelf was against the back wall of the store and there it was, her book! There were half a dozen or so copies, sitting there beside other books about lighthouses and glossy picture books about Lake Superior and northern Michigan. Pleased to confirm that her book was actually there on the shelf, Bertie wandered over to another display and idly picked up a snow globe of the lighthouse, while she looked to see if anyone picked her memoir book off the shelf. She couldn't resist giving the snow globe a gentle shake, conjuring up memories of the stark winters at Whitefish Point. All the other items in the store, however, seemed to be incongruous with what had been their relatively spartan existence at the light station long ago.

The least congested area of the store was around the postcard racks, so Bertie found herself there, looking at several images of the ill-fated *Edmund Fitzgerald* that sank at Whitefish Point, decades after her grandparents had been the lighthouse keepers. A spin of the rack revealed images of the lighthouse in different seasons. She thought that they should carry more postcards of native birds.

One postcard of the lighthouse caught her eye, an image of the lighthouse and its reflection in a huge puddle. The watery reflection was captured with photographic clarity so that when she turned the postcard around, she almost couldn't tell which was the real lighthouse and which was the watery mirage. The reflection was anchored with a darker sky—seemingly to portend an impending storm. This reminded Bertie of what her family was always waiting and watching for at the lighthouse—life-threatening storms.

Turning the postcard over again to the right-side-up view, the reflection of the lighthouse in the temporary pool of snowmelt looked as if the lighthouse were submerged like the shipwrecks beneath the dark waters of Lake Superior just over the dune. This thought caused a memory to surface about one of the many things she learned at her Grandfather Carlson's knee. He told her about the twice-yearly turnover of water in the lake that happened in the fall and again in the spring at just about the time of year the postcard image would have been taken. Her grandfather had gone into detail about why the temperature of the water in the lake caused the water at the bottom to rise and mix with the warmer water at the top to exchange layers. This "turnover" idea captured her imagination as a child. She couldn't help thinking about what else might have been returned to the surface of the water and maybe even end up on the shore... like parts of shipwrecked boats.

Her focus returned to the reflection on the postcard, and her musings were dredging up the long-ago past while at the same time anticipating a future when lighthouse life might also be submerged and forgotten. This place was no longer her home, nor anyone's home. Her grandparents had passed away years ago. The fact that the lighthouse station was now a museum meant that this way of life, her way of life, had truly sunk into the depths of the past. However, her memories were resurfacing upon her return. Some memories were warm and light—her blissful early youth—others were colder and darker—her shattered innocence during wartime. The weather and warfare caused an ill wind *from without* to seep *within* the lighthouse with chilling effects.

Bertie shook off those disturbing thoughts when she suddenly realized that she had missed the second tour and she might miss the third. She almost left without paying for the postcards she had in her hand. She got in line behind the cashier who had only one customer to serve. She might have been impatient for the chatty woman ahead of her to conclude her business of buying several souvenirs including a lighthouse tote bag, except that she was also expressing interest in buying Bertie's memoir that was featured on a small bookstand on the counter. The customer picked up the book and asked the cashier, "Is this a true story?" The cashier shrugged and said, "I'm not sure. It might be one of those haunted lighthouse books." Bertie then felt compelled to interject. "Excuse me. I have it on good authority that every word in that book is true." The customer thanked Bertie for the information and added it to her purchases. Bertie bought her postcards and made her way out of the gift shop working against the wave of tourists from the first tour coming into the busy shop. She had to navigate around a teenage girl who was completely engrossed in reading a book about haunted lighthouses. It was difficult for Bertie to resist the urge to tell the young girl, "Put that silly book down. The *true* stories I could tell you about living here at the light would be *much* more interesting and, I dare say, even spookier."

LIGHTHOUSE KEEPER'S RESIDENCE TOUR
SEPTEMBER 13, 1996
&
TRIGGERED MEMORIES
1917-1918

Docent: *"Welcome to the Whitefish Point lighthouse keeper's residence. My name is Drew and I'll be your guide today. I'm a history major at the University of Michigan and a summer intern here,"* announced the young docent to the dozen or so people lined up outside the house, bracing themselves against the strong wind coming off Lake Superior.

"While this structure is now a museum, typically two families lived in this side-by-side duplex. We will be touring the east side. This side was occupied by the main lighthouse keeper and his family. You will be learning about the duties of lighthouse keepers and their families today. I was interested to learn that one of a lighthouse keeper's stated duties was to take visitors on tours of the station as long as the visitors didn't interfere with the keeper's ability to keep the

light operating. Furthermore, the keeper had to pledge that he—or she—would not receive any fee for admitting visitors to the lighthouses. However, before you ask for a refund of your ticket, remember that I'm just a docent and not an official lighthouse keeper, so you'll have to pay the price of admission, after all. Seriously, thank you for supporting the lighthouse with your visit today."

Bertie looked around to see with whom she was about to share the tour. She noticed a senior citizen wearing an embroidered ball cap from a branch of the military, a couple of women wearing souvenir sweatshirts from other lighthouses, two couples exhibiting varying degrees of interest in what they had paid for, and a family with young children. Doubtless, those parents had promised the excitement of a climb to the top of the tower, if their children could just be patient during the more mundane parts of the tour.

Bertie remembered what lighthouse keepers dreaded most were not curious visitors, but the surprise visits of the official lighthouse inspectors. The first thing the inspector would notice would be the exterior painting job of the lighthouse residence. In addition to being on watch and performing the tasks related to maintaining the light, much of the rest of a lighthouse keeper's time was devoted to three chores—painting, painting again, and doing it all over again.

The inspector's scrutiny of the keeper's painting job could be so exacting as to be absurd. According to the inspector's report, Bertie's grandfather's painting of the kitchen ceiling did not pass muster. Demerit marks were recorded for not having the brushstrokes going all in the same direction.

Perhaps, if Bertie's grandmother had painted the kitchen, the brushstrokes would have been more uniform because she would have brought the same precision to painting the ceiling that she had to brushing and styling Bertie's hair. However, one task her grandmother wasn't allowed to do was painting the tower—not because of the precarious position required, but the concern for propriety. That chore required sitting in a sling high above the ground, and the Light House Service did not want their lady keepers to perch in such an unladylike position.

Bertie thought that the exterior paint job that she was seeing today would certainly pass inspection. The blindingly white paint reflected the sunlight, which had returned after the brief rainstorm. It made Bertie squint—blurring the image and almost erasing the intervening years between the present and the past—as she looked up at the lighthouse keeper's quarters and tower.

Docent: *"The keeper's quarters and the tower date from 1861. It's been restored recently to the era when the Carlson family lived here in the early 1900s. Robert Carlson was the longest-serving lighthouse keeper, stationed here from 1903-1931. I understand that the Carlson's granddaughter, who is still living, believe it or not, provided some authentic family items from their time living here at the lighthouse."*

"Believe it or not she's still living," Bertie parroted the docent's cheeky statement to herself, "and she's not *that* old *and* she's standing right here in line eagerly waiting to walk back into her past." The docent's glib off-hand comment was like a gentle slap on the cheek to keep Bertie in the "here and now." Other than the docent's reference to her advanced age, she didn't mind his long-winded introduction to the tour before they were ushered into the house because it gave her some time to accept her "visitor" status.

Until today, this wasn't a place where Bertie had ever "visited." She had lived here while her maternal grandparents raised her. She rarely called them anything other than Mama and Papa, which her grandparents must have modified at some point to "Mama Anna" and "Papa C" to leave room for the possibility and the *hope* that her parents would one day return: their daughter Cecelia from the Morgan Heights Sanatorium, where she was being treated for TB, and their son-in-law from stateside service at Camp Grayling.

"Before we go inside, just a few ground rules," Drew announced. "Please stay behind the cordoned-off areas of each room, but you're welcome to take photographs and..."

"Is this lighthouse haunted?" blurted the girl with the ghost story book from the gift shop under her arm.

"The short answer is 'It isn't.' The longer answer is "It *absolutely* isn't." Drew didn't seem to have much patience with getting derailed by irrelevant questions and subjects that were off his script. "This is not a ghost tour. My background is in history, and our docent training only covers the facts. Believe me, the facts are much more interesting than legends and myths. People are often fascinated with stories about so-called haunted lighthouses, but..."

"There's a ghost looking out the window!" exclaimed the girl pointing to the house behind Drew.

"I'm sorry to disappoint you again, but that's not a ghost. That's a mannequin," Drew answered somewhat exasperated, glancing at his notes on a small clipboard.

"It's not a man. It's a little girl!" insisted the wide-eyed girl on the tour.

Bertie thought she had seen a ghost, too. It was startling to see the life-size, and fairly life-like, doll complete with the blond sausage curls her grandmother would fashion for her, staring out the window. It was like seeing a reflection of herself, 76 years ago.

"I said 'man-ne-quin,' not 'man,'" Drew explained with an indulgent smile. He spoke directly to the girl, "I'll tell you what. On this tour, I'll tell you more about the little 'ghost' girl you thought you saw in the window. She had a remarkable life here at the lighthouse. You'll like learning about this *real* little girl, Bertha Endress. Her nickname was Bertie and she lived here with her brother and grandparents," Drew said, confident that he had put this matter to rest. "Watch your step as you go up the stairs to the kitchen," he said addressing the group. "The paint on the treads can be slippery after a rainfall."

As Bertie climbed the stairs, she felt a measure of trepidation that wasn't solely related to the slick steps. She was about to enter a time capsule that would trigger feelings of nostalgia and another emotion that she wasn't quite ready to name. As she paused on the landing, she stamped the sand off her shoes as if to root herself in the "here and now" as she stepped into her long-ago past.

Bertie thought the museum staff got it right when they placed the mannequin representing young Bertie as she stood vigil at the window. She had often stood there looking eagerly for visitors to their remote Whitefish Point lighthouse. Some visitors that she hoped and prayed for—her mother and father. Some that she was nervous about—the lighthouse inspectors. Some that she dreaded—the drowned souls. Some that she eagerly anticipated—the "Sky Pilot." And some that she dreamed of accompanying as they came and went—the birds. And some that she was curious about—the new assistant lighthouse keepers—especially the Schroeders—from the time they arrived with their trunks and their accents. The only thing disappointing about their arrival was that they didn't bring any children, which meant more solitary time for her and Bobbie.

Bertie remembered with the clarity of the crystal-clean window out of which the wide-eyed mannequin was staring, a specific time when her feet were planted firmly in that same place. She was looking out the window with Grandfather's binoculars when she spotted an unfamiliar bird. Straining to get as close as possible to see the plumage on the bird's crest, she accidentally clunked the binoculars against the windowpane just as her grandfather entered the kitchen with an empty teacup.

"I know they're not a toy!" Bertie quickly said by way of apology.

"What are you talking about, child?" Papa C asked distractedly as he rummaged through the cupboard for the tin of black tea he always drank to stay alert on his shift."

"I remember you told me that your binoculars are a tool and not a toy. I wasn't playing with them. I was using them." Bertie looked down at the binoculars. They were elegant in design with brass eye cups and leather-covered barrels. The design and weight gave the binoculars the feel of being important to the operation of the lighthouse like most of the contents of the house that were the property of the "US Lighthouse Service."

"I don't mind when you use them for your bird-watching, Bertie, but I don't want your brother to get ahold of them. He's too young to know how to take care of them. You know we are responsible for anything broken—binoculars or even teacups."

"When do you think the inspector will come again?" Bertie asked nervously.

"Oh, it could be anytime soon. He comes about every three months," Papa C said as he checked his pocket-watch ever mindful of his next shift. I'll bet you'll know before I do, given how much time you spend looking out the window for birds. I suppose I should assign you to the post of 'lookout scout.'"

KITCHEN

Docent: *"Although, you can't see any evidence of this in the kitchen, imagine this scene with rescued shipwreck survivors wrapped in blankets sitting here in this very spot to get warm as quickly as possible. Now let me draw your attention to what you can see here in this room. Notice the cupboard here in the kitchen. All the plates, cups, and saucers are labeled 'U.S.L.H.S.," which stands for 'United States Lighthouse Service.' This is symbolic of the fact that although you are visitors today to the lighthouse keeper's home, so, too, in many respects were the lighthouse keeper and his family. Just about everything a lighthouse keeper's family had belonged to the Lighthouse Service. When the lighthouse inspector would arrive, the Carlsons, like all families stationed at a lighthouse, would have to account for every missing piece of china, flat wear, or what-have-you. This gives me another opportunity to remind you that we are guests, so please stay on the hallway runners throughout the home. Follow the traffic pattern as we move from the kitchen, dining room, parlor, and the lighthouse keeper's office to the room devoted to exhibits and upstairs to the bedrooms and, finally, everyone's favorite area of the house, the tower and lantern."*

Bertie had become accustomed to the idea of hundreds of people tramping through her family's former home. Still, it disturbed her to think about the public traipsing up the lighthouse tower stairs and standing near the most important pieces of equipment to the U.S.L.H.S.

Grandfather would roll over in his grave if he knew of the security breach in allowing the everyday public to be admitted to such a sensitive area, vital to national defense, especially during the Great War. Yet, the current part of the tour was about domestic life at the light, so she mustn't get ahead of herself, not even in her thoughts. Bertie followed the crowd to the kitchen like a queue of ants following a scent trail.

While standing in the kitchen, Bertie found that the years were unspooling to a time when she had stood at her grandmother's elbow eager to help and asked her grandmother why she was sprinkling a concoction of ground cinnamon and cloves here and there around the kitchen. Mama Anna answered, "To give those pesky ants 'hot foot!'" Bertie wondered if the person in front of her in the column heard the single chuff of her laughter when she thought about whether her grandmother would have wanted to give all these interlopers the same treatment. Mama Anna, also, would have told them to stick to the hallway runners.

Docent: *"Anna Carlson here is hard at work in the kitchen,"* Drew said as he pointed to a second mannequin. This one represented Bertie's grandmother. *"Every member of a lighthouse family had a role to play in keeping the light. Even though the keeper took the oath to serve in this difficult job, it was understood that his family was a critical support system for the whole operation. Anna Carlson was also busy raising their two grandchildren. I'm not sure why they were raising their young grandchildren, instead of them being raised by their daughter, but I digress."*

It was painful for Bertie to remember that not *every* member of the Carlson family was part of the lighthouse keeper's support system. Well, not part of *her* support system, anyway. Her parents were largely absent. It was best to remember that she and her younger brother were very well cared for by Grandmother and Grandfather Carlson. In most ways, she and her brother Bobbie lacked for nothing.

Even though the tour brought up a lot of good memories of life at the light, Bertie couldn't completely suppress all the complicated feelings she had about that singular and very solitary life. This was especially hard to do when she was standing in the kitchen and found herself feeling the same age as her nature-watching mannequin on the day she turned 8 years old.

She held that dear memory close, almost as if she were holding a snow globe protectively in her hands, shaking it gently to jog her memory and recreate the swirl of snow and wind that circled her that day—the day that she had begged Papa C to take her out into the woods to help him choose the Christmas tree. She didn't know at first that he was teasing her when he said he couldn't leave the lighthouse without someone 'on duty.' "Then I will build a snowman," young Bertie countered, "to stand watch in your place."

Papa C smiled and said, "Well, some days are so slow here that a snowman might as well stand in for me.

How about you go outside and make that man from last night's freshly fallen snow?" He told her by the time she went outside and made his "second-in-command," he would be ready to go with her to the woods. When he came outside to make good on his promise, he gave her an old pipe for the new "assistant lightkeeper."

Her grandfather added, "Lightkeepers need a pastime to keep them awake, but I would hate to start the young frozen fellow on a habit that could jeopardize his health. Smoking might very well be his undoing." That comment made him chuckle to himself but made Bertie's brow crinkle with worry, so Papa C added, "There is no chance of him melting, but there is a chance of us ending up as frozen as he is. Let's make quick work of getting that tree."

As they trudged through the snow, the ribbon of smoke from Papa C's pipe and the familiar smell tethered Bertie to her grandfather's side as much as the strong grip he had on her small hand. Her fingers were doubly insulated by the mitten knitted by her grandmother and her grandfather's work gloves. On the way back from the woods, Bertie noticed his gloves were sticky with sap from the freshly felled Balsam Fir he dragged behind them, the branches erasing their steps in the snow like a big paintbrush.

Even though it was bitterly cold as they returned, the sight of the chimney of the house and the plume of pipe smoke blowing over her head gave her the illusion of warmth. She loved the smell mixed with Papa C's Prince Albert's "soft and sweet" scented tobacco. When he smoked outside the smell wasn't just an odor but took on the mystique of an aroma. When he smoked indoors, however, the smell was cloying and a bit nauseating. Bertie could still recite the advertisement on the 10-cent tin of Prince Albert tobacco. *"The national joy-smoke. Prince Albert brand can't bite your tongue nor any man's. The patented process removes the sting."* Bertie was able to commit the slogan on the tobacco tin to memory because every scrap of reading material, whether it was a recipe lying on the kitchen counter or an advertisement on the pantry shelf, might be worth memorizing. Being raised at a light station in the middle of nowhere, reciting a quaint slogan was akin to reciting poetry.

Bertie recalled that Papa C was much more relaxed when he smoked. Perhaps, because his brand of tobacco "removed the sting." His personality, altered by the "joy-smoke," was a welcome change in his disposition, or so grandmother said, from the furtive restlessness that came as much with the job as the uniform did.

As they got closer to the house, little Bertie thought the dogs, the rambunctious littermates Beacon and Bell, looked like they were smoking, too, with the warm breath from their snouts suspended in the frigid air. Bertie could see the red scarf Mama Anna had given her to wrap around the snowman's neck. The stout fellow also served as a weather vane as the scarf blew straight out in the bitter breeze off Lake Superior. Grandfather told Bertie to run ahead and catch the scarf before it blew away into the woods.

Grandmother looked out the window and saw Bertie running toward the house alone without her grandfather and she hurried to the door worried that something had happened to him. Her anxiousness coupled with her grandfather's restlessness, had made Bertie attuned to the "radio frequency" in the house, where sometimes tension could be a welcome intermission from the more often than not monotonous life at the light. Later, Bertie would realize why the vigils her grandmother kept at the house were so fraught. It was possible that Grandmother never really got over the time when Grandfather and his brother did not return home when expected.

It was easy to get worried here at Whitefish Point and scolding someone, usually Grandfather, followed and resolved Mama Anna's anxiousness. Sometimes, Mama Anna left the scolding of Papa C and Bertie to Tomte, a spirit being who "lived with them" at the lightkeeper's house and was as much a source of fascination to the impressionable Bertie as were the Schroeders who shared the other half of their divided lighthouse at that time.

Tomte's presence, in Swedish lore, protected a family as long as they were industrious and, therefore, worthy of his elfin help. Her Swedish-born grandmother would not hesitate to invoke Tomte's name to make Bertie mind, do her chores, and be respectful so he would continue to dwell amongst them and protect the family. Bertie came to understand Tomte as a complicated fellow who was a bit capricious in doling out his favors.

While growing up, Bertie didn't hear much about Tomte during the spring and summer months. Apparently, he slept under the floor boards and didn't rouse himself until the drear of the darkening days before the winter solstice made their increasingly solitary existence a breeding ground for imagination. During these times, Tomte seemed to be at Mama Anna's beck and call.

"Bertie, how could you keep Tomte waiting until dusk to come home? He will have to do more cleaning and cooking while we sleep because you weren't home to help me in the kitchen. Who knows what mischief he will be up to because you did not respect his time?"

"Mama Anna," Bertie responded. "You'll just need to make the porridge with the butter he likes, and he will forgive me."

On that particular day, Grandmother's response was tamped down by the sound of Grandfather stomping up the outside steps to the kitchen. As he opened the door, the tree shielded him from Grandmother's threat, "I should give you both porridge *without* butter for your dinner," Mama Anna shouted over her shoulder from the stove. Yet, she couldn't help but smile at the sight of that perfect tree. Papa C then leaned it against the wall, careful not to have it topple forward onto the pastry table in the center of the kitchen. He used a whisk broom to brush off the snow from his coat and pants, a habit that made Mama Anna frosty and she winced at the indoor snow shower. How many times had she told him to do that out on the stoop? He then shrugged off his coat, hung it up on one of the hooks over the radiator, and went to pull out a kitchen chair to sit down to pull off his boots.

"Robert, not that chair," said Anna. He looked puzzled and a bit annoyed but pulled out another chair to shuck off his boots. Papa C didn't seem curious about why he couldn't sit in the first chair. Bertie, however, was curious so she bent down to look under the table to discover a lumpy something wrapped in a dish towel sitting on the seat. "Tomte?" Bertie thought with a start. Mama Anna gently took her by the shoulders to lift her gaze from underneath the table and instructed her to put her mittens on the radiator to dry.

"The tree is bigger than I expected, Robert," Anna said looking at the tree as if it were an uninvited guest. "Will it clear the ceiling in the parlor?" Anna asked skeptically.

"I expect it will. But if it doesn't, I can chop off a bit from the bottom of the trunk. I'm glad that Schroeder made me a new handle for my axe the other day," Robert said as he resumed vigorously brushing the snow off the bottom of his pant legs.

"He's turning out to be handy after all?" Anna asked.

"He's handy alright," Robert added oblivious to Anna's icy facial expression as she looked at the puddles on her kitchen floor, "but the real test will be when the shipping lanes open again in the spring. The upkeep around here is one thing, but tending the light is a whole other thing entirely."

DINING ROOM

Docent: *"The table here is set with the official Lighthouse Service china. Anna Carlson was from a Swedish family who immigrated and settled in Chicago. She probably longed to make the foods from her childhood, but what was in her pantry would have been restricted to the rations delivered to the lighthouse, supplemented by what the Carlsons grew in their garden, berries they picked, or whatever Robert Carlson brought home from fishing or hunting."*

"There are only four places at the table. Did the Carlsons ever have visitors at this remote location?" asked a woman who had been leaning precariously over the rope to take photos of the contents on the table.

Docent: *"The Carlsons had a daughter and twin boys but they would have been adults by the time the Carlsons moved here. It was the daughter's children who were raised here. Usually, the Carlson's dining room was a private place for the family of four. But Anna Carlson also had to feed the men who came to repair the cribs (or jetties), the submarine bell, or anything that keeper Carlson, or the assistant lighthouse keeper, or she couldn't fix on their own. They also, from time to time, had the Coast Guard men, who came from the Vermilion Station on rescue or training missions, and a group of maintenance workers known as 'The Boys.' Or 'The Creosote Boys' as they were sometimes called, ate the biggest breakfasts of all, but then they did have to stand in cold water all morning to shore up the jetty buffeted by Superior's waves day in and day out. And, of course, every great while they had to take care of and feed any survivors of shipwrecks who would be first brought here."*

Bertie stifled a chuckle when the docent mentioned "The Creosote Boys." Those men used sticky creosote to waterproof the wood used at the lighthouse station for pilings for the jetty, and so, of course, they were splattered with creosote when they came in to eat. The family could smell them coming and had to open the windows wide in the dining room and leave them open until midnight.

The creosote smelled like oil smoke, which might be a welcome odor now because the sterile museum house was, sadly, absent of any odor. With an even stronger whiff of nostalgia, Bertie remembered more pleasant smells from childhood from the invisible apparitions of steam coming from the soup on the old Eureka stove to the enticing aroma of bread baking in the oven—haunting every corner of the house. Those aromas were like a siren call to the "The Creosote Boys," and brought them tumbling into the house eager to squeeze in to take seats at Mama Anna's dining room table while Bertie and her brother listened to their banter from the kitchen table where Mama Anna fed them.

Bertie was happy to remember "The Creosote Boys" and how they eagerly ate Mama Anna's food, but she also recalled a much different dinner occasion when only three of their family members, minus her grandfather, sat at the table for the evening meal. Now many years later, she was reminded of the reason for the pointedly vacant spot at the table when Bertie noticed the stylish haircut of the young girl in front of her on the tour—the one with a penchant for reading ghost stories. That impressionable girl would have been thrilled to know that she had conjured up the ghost of Bertie's grandfather with the casual flip of her blond shingled hair. Her grandfather's absence from the dining room table was precipitated by Bertie's decision, with Mama Anna's consent, to get a smart new hairstyle that was then fashionable with teenage girls.

Bertie and Mama Anna had gone shopping with friends in Newberry. The closest town of any size to the lighthouse. Before they left for town, her grandfather most likely took no notice of what Bertie was wearing, but he took it for granted that when she returned, she would still look like his granddaughter with her long locks. However, when Bertie and Mama Anna returned, Bertie was proudly sporting a new haircut. Papa C was so shocked by the sight of her cropped hair, that he lost his hold on his tea cup, and it shattered—shrilly speaking for him when he could not. From the perspective of adulthood, Bertie could now understand that her new appearance had truly startled her grandfather and probably made him feel as if he lost his firm grasp on his granddaughter's childhood.

Earlier that memorable day, Bertie had left the lighthouse with her waist-length tresses but returned with a flapper's bob. Her shocked grandfather quickly became her stern grandfather. His slack-jawed surprise had silenced him for only a brief bit and then he delivered an angry diatribe ending with, "What were you thinking, Anna?!! First, it's a modern haircut, and then it's a modern attitude. Next, it'll be a modern lifestyle—not in keeping with our Swedish way of life and traditions!" Bertie moved her hand reflexively to her wispy strands, remembering how she had pulled at the ends of her newly clipped hair as if she could lengthen her shorn hair and shorten her grandfather's spittle-punctuated speech.

After her grandfather finished pontificating, he left the place he had occupied on center-stage in the dining room and exited to the fog signal building. He did not return for dinner that night choosing to eat at the Coast Guard Station. Grandmother wasn't flustered in the least as she went about her business preparing for dinner as usual. However, she did need to let the dogs out in the chilly weather, since Grandfather had only let *himself* out. She had to return inside in just a few minutes because she heard the phone ringing. She hastily removed her gloves to lift the receiver but dropped the earpiece because her hands were slick from the cornstarch she routinely put in her winter gloves to keep them from stretching. The bell-shaped receiver swung back and forth on its cord like the pendulum of a clock.

In a blink, Bertie's thoughts were transported back even further in her memory than her teenage years to a memory from early in her childhood. She recalled that her grandfather had dropped that same telephone earpiece— just after receiving some sort of startling news. When her grandfather told her grandmother what he learned from that long ago phone call, Bertie couldn't remember what he said to Mama Anna at the time, but she did remember her grandmother's anguished exclamations of sorrow. Because Grandfather had stomped out of the house in protest to Bertie and Mama Anna's collusion to cut her hair, he wasn't at the dining room table that evening to converse with Grandmother, so Bertie took the opportunity to ask about that long-ago distressing phone call.

"I just had the strangest memory," the teenaged Bertie announced tentatively as she reflexively reached to twist a lock of her hair before remembering that her hair was much too short for that previously calming habit.

"Oh?" her grandmother said distractedly as she carefully placed the newly washed plates, cups and saucers in the glass-fronted china cabinet.

"There was another time when you and Papa C were both very upset when you got surprising news of some kind," Bertie ventured as she handed a clean serving bowl to her grandmother.

"I hope you aren't letting your grandfather's stormy behavior get to you, dear. For a man trained to be ready for a disaster at any time, he makes such a fuss over the little things sometimes," Mama Anna said as she closed the cabinet door and turned the small skeleton key to secure the latch.

"My memory is that he was upset, but it couldn't have been over something little. I think he received very bad news, but I don't know what it was. I would have been about five years old, I think. Do you remember an important phone call that would have caused Papa C to drop the earpiece?"

"I certainly do, Bertie. I had no idea that you would remember that, though," Mama Anna recalled as she sank into her chair at the table with the weight of the memory. "We did receive news of a tragedy, but you were too little to be told about it at the time."

"And now?" Bertie asked hopefully.

"There was a tragedy that hit much too close to home," Mama Anna said as her hand moved to her chest as if to quell an errant heartbeat.

"It happened close to our home here?" Bertie asked.

"I mean that the tragedy involved family members," Mama Anna said shuddering. "I've always thought that in times of tragedy, hopeful disbelief causes the ticking of the clock to somehow stand still between the minutes 'before the bad news' and the minutes 'after the bad news.'"

"Mama Anna, what *was* the bad news you received? I remember you screamed and cried." Bertie moved to the chair next to Mama Anna where her grandfather would normally sit.

"It all started about three weeks before that phone call, which would have been the summer of 1915. My sister Laura called from Chicago to announce that she was going on an outing with her friend Cora and they wanted me to go along. They were going to take a boat from Chicago to Michigan City in Indiana. The boat, a luxury liner actually, was chartered to give workers a special excursion to go picnicking and such. I thought I would never forget the name of that boat, but it escapes me just now....Oh! I remember it now! The Eastland. The SS Eastland!"

"Did you get to go?" Bertie asked, forgetting momentarily that this story might not have a happy ending.

"No, I didn't. Your grandfather said that I couldn't go. I was boiling mad about it at the time," Mama Anna picked up a fork from the table setting to polish. "I was a city-bred girl from Chicago and the stark loneliness of our postings over the years was...appalling. When we were posted to Whitefish Point, I had to sacrifice friends and the more interesting life we had at the Marquette Station. And then I had to pass up a trip back home to Chicago to visit my sister."

"I know how difficult it would be to change Papa C's mind," Bertie commiserated as she tried to view her recently shorn image in a newly polished spoon.

"There was no persuading him, so I had to relent. Once I cooled down, I wasn't as angry as I was disappointed. However, I soon had to put my disappointment aside because I found myself busy feeding a crew of men who had arrived unexpectedly," Mama Anna said as she sighed and reached for the utensils from the next place setting. "That's what a lighthouse keeper's family does, of course."

"But who called? What happened?" Bertie asked while she glanced at the telephone mounted on the dining room wall—almost expecting it to ring.

"It was your grandfather's brother, Carl. He worked near Chicago at the time. He called with the horrible news about the sinking of the *SS Eastland*. The ship's manifest was published in the *Chicago Tribune* with the names of all the passengers who had perished onboard and my sister's name was on it!"

"I don't understand. Aunt Laura is alive and well!" Bertie exclaimed pointing to a family photo on top of the china cabinet.

"Yes, of course, but her name was listed as having perished even though she never boarded the boat. You see, her friend Cora was late that morning getting to the dock. When Cora finally arrived in a taxi cab, they'd missed the all-aboard whistle. Laura was fuming mad."

"You told me about her quick-rising temper when you were growing up," Bertie recalled.

"Yes, but in this case, Laura's anger disappeared quickly when she and Cora were standing on the dock and watched the boat suddenly list to one side and roll over right there at the dock," Mama Anna paused and then added, "Witnessing a shipwreck is something that you never forget."

"Poor Aunt Laura and her friend! But they were fortunate," Bertie said.

"Fortunate, yes, but forever burdened by the memory of those horrible sights...and the sounds." My sister always could remember things in greater detail than most people, but that ability turned out to be a curse," Mama Anna said shaking her head sympathetically.

"What do you mean about that being a curse?" Bertie asked.

"Laura told me that she could never forget the sound of a piano crashing into everything in its path as it careened across the tilting promenade deck," Mama Anna remembered. Then she rose to look for something in the drawer of the china cabinet where she stored correspondence from her family. "Here it is! Laura wrote about what she experienced that day in this letter. 'If there were a sound when time seemed to slow down in a tragedy, it would be the ghastly sound of all the piano strings ringing at once. No music. Just misery,'" Mama Anna read as she dropped into her seat.

"Since the boat hadn't left the dock, were most of the passengers able to be rescued from the boat?" Bertie asked as she absentmindedly emptied the turntable of its contents in the center of the table.

"No, Bertie," Mama Anna said nodding her head decisively. "Over 800 souls drowned that morning, but by the grace of God, *not* your Aunt Laura and her *blessedly* tardy friend Cora."

"How did you discover that Aunt Laura *wasn't* on the boat?"

"As we were still trying to hold on to our disbelief that Laura had perished on the shipwreck, your grandfather reached for the dangling receiver and replaced it on the hook in shock without remembering that his brother was still on the line. Then the phone rang again jumpstarting our grief anew. Your grandfather picked up the earpiece again and I heard him ask, 'Who *is* this?'"

"Who was it?" Bertie asked scooting forward in her chair.

"My sister Laura!" Mama Anna said as she reached across the table to place her hand on Bertie's. "Your grandfather didn't believe it was her voice because he thought that she was dead. Stunned, he just handed the earpiece to me and slowly lowered himself into a chair with his head in his hands while I screamed and cried with every emotion that I had ever experienced up to that point in my life. It's no wonder you remembered that day...even if you didn't know what it was all about," Mama Anna said as she replaced all the items back onto the pedestal in the center of the table as if to "right the ship."

"What do you know about *why* the ship sank?" Bertie asked.

"I never really wanted to know anything more about it other than that my sister was spared by fate, by the hand of God, or both. Otherwise, it's just ghoulish fascination, if you ask me," Mama Anna said as she stood up and smoothed her white apron as if to wipe the slate clean.

PARLOR

Docent: *"Most of the Carlson's furnishings came from their previous lighthouse-keeping assignments at Bayfield and Marquette. I believe the radio you see here would have been provided by the Lighthouse Service in the 1920s, but the Carlsons probably purchased the Estey pump organ on their own. Since this room was the heart of family life, especially during the chilliest months, these fixtures were vitally important. The radio provided news of the outside world. These sources of entertainment and education were certainly supplemented with games such as cribbage and contact bridge."*

"Excuse me. I'm so sorry that my son is so squirmy. He's trying to get away from me to play with that mannequin over there," said the mother who had a wrist-lock on her restless 4-year-old, perhaps a couple years younger than the ever-grinning Pinocchio-like mannequin. "By the way, how did the young children of lighthouse keepers entertain themselves?"

Docent: *"Children often had to rely on their own resources for entertainment. In fact, I read a memoir of a lighthouse keeper in which he recounted that the lighthouse inspector had ordered the removal of a swing that the keeper had attached to a tree limb because the children's feet had worn away the grass underneath it. Sad, but true. So, siblings here at the light station were a lifeline. Also, the children of married assistant lighthouse keepers became treasured friends. However, sometimes it was just the two grandchildren here at the lighthouse, Bertie and her younger brother Bobbie. Toys they would have played with in the early 20th century were tinker toys, tin soldiers, and dolls, of course. I probably shouldn't admit this, but this make-believe boy is a source of entertainment for us, the docent staff, that is. One of the docents is afraid of the mannequin because she thinks he looks like those dolls that scare people in horror movies. We like to move him about the home to surprise our fellow docents. Please don't tell the Shipwreck Museum director, though!"*

Bertie liked to think of her brother's mannequin as a source of amusement for the docents since she had had to tolerate a lot of her brother's antics when they were growing up here. The docents had gotten the pose for "Bobbie" just right. The mannequin looked like he had just played a joke on her and was so convulsed with laughter that he had rocked back on his haunches with the debilitating delight of it.

Their age difference meant that Bertie had more memories of playing alongside Bobbie than really playing together. However, the two of them liked listening to the radio in the evening with their grandparents, whether or not they were truly interested in any given program. Just the sound of other voices—a change from their usual quartet—was welcome. Bertie remembered that the only radio station they could receive for some time was KDKA from Pittsburgh.

Since they lived at least 300 miles north of anywhere and everywhere, why not listen to a broadcast from Pittsburgh?

The radio on display was of a different vintage than the one they had used. Bertie was distracted by the things in the room that weren't used by the Carlsons. These strange objects awakened her to the reality that traveling back "home" would prove ultimately impossible. Other objects, particularly the ones that she didn't have or didn't choose to contribute to the house museum, also distracted Bertie by their absence.

She was particularly fond of a certain toy that had been made just for her and for that reason she just couldn't part with for the museum. She did wonder, however, if she should have parted with it because she had mixed feelings about how the toy had played with her emotions then, and still did now. The toy was a birthday present from the couple that lived in the other half of the lighthouse—the assistant lighthouse keeper and his wife, Mr. and Mrs. Schroeder. It was that same Christmas when Bertie first helped her grandfather to get the tree from the woods. Apparently while they were out in the woods, the Schroeders delivered the gift. Mama Anna barely had time to conceal it beneath the kitchen table on a chair and cover it with a dish towel when Bertie and Papa C came in from getting the Christmas tree. Her birthday came so close to Christmas that her brother always complained that it was unfair that she seemed to get more Christmas presents than he did. Unlike Papa C's hunting dogs, Bobbie's indoor yapping would not be trained out of him for some time.

That Christmas season, as she was sitting on the parlor floor rug, Bertie finally got to unwrap the gift. It was more like an unveiling than an opening of a present. Not only because of the dishcloth drape but because the gift was a piece of art and craftsmanship fashioned completely out of wood. It was the dearest gift. It had a propeller on top like a miniature ceiling fan. The toy immediately captured Bobbie's imagination and he needed to be brought to heel by Papa C so that he would not be able to grab hold of it while Bertie was still admiring the simple beauty of the unusual object.

The propeller was attached to a stem affixed to the base through a hole in the top of an archway which was shaped like the outline of a stylized tree—much like how a child would draw a Christmas tree with symmetrical branches. Inside the shelter of the tree (on a disc that spun when you set the propeller on top in motion) were small carved figures that looked like tiny clothespin pegs. Bertie recognized that the peg people represented the Holy Family in the manger. The surrounding figures confirmed that the scene was the nativity with sheep carved to give them a curly wool texture, a shepherd holding a crook, and an angel watching over the family. Bertie's grandfather took a close look at the toy and soon explained that the tiny recessed cups on the base were for mounting small candles. He and Mama Anna found some candles and placed them into the cups.

When lit, the candles produced a heat that made the propeller of the tree turn and if that wasn't fascinating enough, Bertie's eyes shone as it dawned on her that the angel looked just like the guardian angel she had sometimes conjured up in her dreams. Above all, she was flattered that Mr. and Mrs. Schroeder would give her such a unique toy and that they trusted she was old enough to appreciate and care for such a delicate gift. She didn't realize until months later that the Schroeders had also trusted in her naivete and how the gift would make Bertie trust *them*.

Bertie returned to the here and now, after admiring in her mind's eye, the memorable gift of the German Christmas pyramid, when she realized that the tour group had moved on down the hallway to her grandfather's office.

Bertie, alone now in the parlor, audibly "tsked" and shook her head because, even though she was lost in thought, she had been vaguely aware of the docent's ongoing presentation and that he had failed to mention the *most* important item in the parlor—a thick-walled wooden chest of dove-tail box construction with heavy brass fittings.

Looking to verify that she was alone, Bertie took the liberty of unhooking the dark maroon velvet rope from the stanchion and snuck into the parlor exhibition space, reattaching the hook behind her. If the next tour group caught her, she could freeze in a pose like a mannequin. After all, she now looked like the mannequin of the old woman in the kitchen. Though she wouldn't take the risk to play the organ, she could furtively open the rustic bookcase to see if the treasure within the box was still there. She approached the chest with the same excitement she did as a child when she would watch Mama Anna open the box to reveal the precious contents. Dozens of books on loan. Those books would be *all theirs* for a few months to read and to travel vicariously wherever the stories took them—all across the world.

Bertie used to think it was just like Christmas when the deliveries came. The Reverend William Law was a much-anticipated "Jultomten," which was the Swedish equivalent of Santa Claus. The Reverend made it to the light station, not once, but three times a year. He came on a U.S.L.H.S. supply boat from which he would disembark from the tender ship

with the portable Lighthouse Establishment libraries—each
case with its specific number emblazoned onto the outside.
Reverend Law, or "The Sky Pilot," as sailors referred to him,
wasn't simply bringing entertainment to the lighthouse
with the traveling libraries. He was bringing the "Gospel of
Humanity," as he called his mission.

Coming back to the present, Bertie experienced a
frisson of alarm when she noticed some gaps on the shelves
of the library box that should have held about 50 books
nestled shoulder-to-shoulder. She checked the list that
remained affixed to the inside of one of the cabinet doors,
but the books had not been dutifully "checked out." They
had gone missing with no date or name associated with the
disappearance. In Bertie's experience, any lost or "injured"
book had to be accounted for and replaced. Then with a
sigh of relief, she realized she was no longer responsible for
discrepancies in the inventory. She did, however, notice titles
that made her smile in recognition and remembrance—hours
of pleasure reading Gene Stratton Porter's *The Harvester*
and *Michael O'Halloran,* and Chester Reed's bird guides.
A Bible was always included in each box, but the Carlsons
chose to read their Swedish Bible—the illustrations of which
had scared Bertie as a child. Bertie remembered Mama
Anna scanning the titles in the newly delivered box for the
Swedish romance series she enjoyed. It was as if Mama
Anna were standing still on a depot platform searching
a slowing train for the first glimpse of a beloved familiar
through the compartment windows.

Bertie opened the bird guide that was in this
particular box. She opened its cover and was pleased to see
the official Light House Establishment bookplate affixed to

the inside cover of the book. Suddenly, she experienced a sense of alarm in real-time when she heard the back door to the kitchen creak open to admit the next group of visitors. She had no time to close the bookcase doors, but she did indulge in some mischief and placed her brother's mannequin in a different place—this time in a seated position directly in front of the bookbox. That might pique the interest of the docents in talking about the lighthouse libraries, or, at the very least, keep them guessing about who had moved the boy mannequin this time.

Once again on the visitor side of the rope, her eyes lighted on the "Edison Standard" phonograph in the room. Bertie could almost hear the words of a certain song that had come out of the speaker horn, which was pointed in the direction of the kitchen now, just as it was way back when. From Bertie's vantage point on the carpet runner, she could look one way and see her grandmother's mannequin at work in the kitchen and look the other way and see her grandfather's mannequin at work at his desk in his office. There was a time when her grandparents were as uncommunicative as their doppelgängers were now at opposite ends of the house.

The source of the distance between her grandparents was a visit to friends in which one of the ladies there, as Bertie heard Mama Anna say, "made too much a fuss over Robert." Perhaps, Papa C had also made a bit of a fuss over that woman. In any event, she was so irritated with Papa C that she didn't speak a single word to him for weeks. What finally broke the silence and brokered the peace between them was a clever move deployed by *Captain* Carlson.

He had gone to a music store in Sault Ste. Marie and bought a record with a song that spoke just the right lyrics to communicate with his wife through the charged atmosphere of conflict. Bertie could still see him enter the parlor where she was practicing the organ and signal to her to stop playing. Bertie was only too happy to oblige him. She watched him almost tiptoe over to the phonograph with a package under his arm. He slipped the new record out of its sleeve and placed it gingerly on the turntable spindle. Just before he put the tonearm over the disc, he looked at Bertie with a finger to his lips and made a conspiratorial "Shh!" to keep his maneuver a secret. As the needle made its first revolution, the Captain made his retreat to the safety of the signal horn building to await the result of his tactical mission.

The song's lyrics hit so close to home that Bertie worried that the pointed message of the song might make the situation between her grandparents worse. However, her grandfather's message was received well and harmony was restored as was demonstrated by the meal Mama Anna prepared that night. She made one of Papa C's favorite Swedish dishes with some of the rations she had been keeping in reserve for just such an occasion. As they ate, and all seemed normal again, Bertie could not help but run those lyrics silently through her head.

Mother hasn't spoken to Father
Since she found a hair upon his coat—
And a savory little note—
That some other lady wrote—
Now poor father—he's the goat.
And now it's getting cold around the house!

LIGHTHOUSE KEEPER'S OFFICE

The tour continued and Bertie was now several steps and stages behind. She had missed the docent's presentation in her grandfather's office and whatever questions the visitors might have been inspired to ask when they saw the very life-like mannequin of lightkeeper Robert Carlson sitting at his desk. The sight of her "grandfather," with a pen in his hand, perhaps just before recording an entry into the daily log book, triggered one of Bertie's eavesdropping memories.

Being here in this room, which had been faithfully restored to her grandparent's time of service. Bertie's memories of this space were revealing themselves to be as intact as log book entries. In this particular memory, Grandfather's actual logbook was the source of friction between her grandparents.

Grandfather must have noticed as he entered the kitchen that day so many years back, that Mama Anna was baking up a storm, but it wasn't her usual "baking day." At first, this seemed like a welcome change of routine, because more baked goods in the larder would surely be something pleasant to anticipate. There she was with all her tools—the sifter, rolling pin, and bowl. He could see and hear the rigor of the enterprise—the trigger action of the sifter, the furious whipping of the ingredients, and the vigorous flattening of the dough. That was all normal, but something had to have happened to cause his wife to not only change "baking day" to today, but do so with such fervor. Yet, Grandfather was also somewhat agitated and was on his own mission as he entered Grandmother's territory.

"Anna, I know you've wanted to get to know the Schroeders better, particularly Mrs. Schroeder. Did you have them over for tea, by any chance, when I went fishing yesterday?" Robert said as he sat down at the kitchen table and placed his closed logbook in front of him.

"No, I didn't. Did you want me to ask them over? You haven't seemed too keen on getting to know them better," Anna said without slowing her tempo with the rolling pin.

"I'm not eager to get to know *them* better, but I *am* anxious to know what *Mr.* Schroeder is about," Robert said, frowning such that his handsome face was altered by concern.

"About?" asked Anna as she began to clean bits of sticky dough off her rolling pin.

"I mean 'up to,'" Robert said scratching his head in puzzlement.

"It seems he is 'up to' going up the lighthouse stairs to relieve you from taking every shift," Anna said while wiping her hands on a tea towel that had been part of her wedding trousseau.

"I'm not sure he *is* taking all his shifts." Robert surmised as he grasped his chin in thought.

"Really? And you can't ask him? Men are so finicky about the questions they will ask one another," Anna said shaking her head. "Why was it that you thought I had invited them for tea?" Anna asked as she placed the sheet of dough in the pie plate like carefully arranging the bottom sheet on a bed.

"It seems *someone* opened up my log book and left it open on a different page than the one on which I made my entry yesterday," Robert said as he tapped his index finger firmly on the cover.

"That 'someone' was me. I didn't think you would mind because you don't write anything of a personal nature in the logbooks. Not a single personal reference," Anna said accusingly.

He was at a loss as to how this routine task could have been the cause of the shifting winds between them. Robert's logbook entries were dry and terse, yet they simply spoke to the tedium of most days, interrupted by the terror of a few other days—year in and year out.

"I think you spend more time at your desk deciding what *not* to write, instead of what *to* write," Anna ventured as she vigorously rolled out the dough for the top crust.

"Anna, it's not a diary, it's a logbook," Robert sharply responded. "There are guidelines affixed to the front of each logbook that spell out exactly what kind of information to include and how to record it." Robert opened the logbook to the first page. "It says right here, 'In keeping the journal, two pages are to be used for one month. The events of the day must be written on one line across both pages. If carefully written, one line will be found sufficient,'" Robert read and then closed the logbook and turned his attention to Anna's rolling pin barometer, the "to-ing and fro-ing" of which could be used to determine the pressure of the atmosphere and to forecast the weather *inside* the lighthouse.

"Anna, you're raising a squall with that flour. Tell me what's wrong," Robert pleaded.

Anna put down her rolling pin, wiped her hands on her apron, and then hesitated before she spoke. "Our boys left home—left the lighthouse—for work in the mines and military duty and you didn't see fit to record that in your logbook for that date. *Don't* read the logbook instructions to me again. *Other* lighthouse keepers enter all sorts of detail into their logbooks about their family's lives and the comings and goings of everyone, and you know it."

"But that's not how it's supposed to be done," Robert countered.

"It's like you've forgotten Robert and Carl," Anna said as she practically twisted the tea towel into a knot of frustration.

"That's not fair. I think about them every day. I've even written a letter to the..." Robert suddenly censored himself, stopping just short of completing his sentence that obviously had something to do with their boys.

Being in the presence of the handsome white-haired mannequin of Captain Carlson in his official navy-blue uniform—minus the cap hanging on the coat rack—also created the illusion that her grandfather had just refrained from finishing his last sentence. Bertie's thoughts were brought back to the present momentarily by the glare of the late morning sun shining through the window of her grandfather's office. The angle of the light revealed the dust motes and they seemed as suspended in the air as was Bertie's memory of her grandfather's unfinished revelation. Looking at the back of her "grandfather" as he sat in his office swivel chair, Bertie felt the greatest emotional shudder yet from this strange "family reunion" tour visit. This was all a bit unnerving and Bertie would have preferred to avoid the memories this tableau evoked for her.

She found that these thoughts rendered her as immovable in this room as was the mannequin. Now that her tour group cluster had moved on to the exhibit room, she would have time to regroup. Just beyond the office, there were several display cases with archival items, like her grandfather's logbooks and the brass implements associated with lighthouse keeper duties—the wick box and oil cans and such. There was even a bellows-operated fog signal horn in one of the display cases. Bertie had supplied some of the items for these frozen-in-time displays—like items in the glass bubble of a paperweight. However, she hadn't been consulted as much about what would be contained in the display cases as she was about the items for the domestic side of life at the light.

Bertie readily acknowledged that the museum professionals knew much more about the operational side of the lighthouse than she did. There was, however, a piece of correspondence that she had had in her possession for decades that she hesitated to provide for one of the museum's display cases. The item, a mere piece of paper, the nature of which was at once an official piece of correspondence and a deeply personal one, crackled with significance. This piece of paper was a letter to the Lighthouse Board and it was the source of the biggest row Bertie had ever overheard between her grandparents.

Bertie was still unsure whether she should have shared the letter with the archivists. She truly had wrestled with the decision to provide this piece of information from midway through her grandfather's long and distinguished career. It was a moral dilemma, really, about sharing information that was never intended to be a part of the official lighthouse records. It represented, to some extent, a lapse in judgment on the part of her grandfather. He had made a decision that could have cost him his career, his marriage, and even his life, without ever consulting her grandmother, who had, as far as Bertie knew, always been his partner in everything up to that point.

Feeling the weight of having decided to supply the letter to the museum, Bertie sat down on the steps that accessed the upstairs directly from the back of her grandfather's office. This was just about the same place on the stairs where she was perched as a little girl while listening to a private conversation between her grandparents. When it was discovered that Bertie had heard every word of the argument, Mama Anna said, "Små kannor har stora öron." *Little pitchers have big ears.* Mama Anna was so angry that she couldn't decide with whom she was most upset—her granddaughter or her husband. Bertie and her grandfather didn't know either.

It had been her fault that the content of her grandfather's letter was exposed. That long ago afternoon, Bertie had brought a hot cup of tea from the kitchen to the office for Papa C, but on the way down the hallway, her brother Bobbie had startled her by blowing a harmonica in her ear. She squawked and barely managed to calm the waters of the teacup as some of it sloshed over the rim and into the saucer. The hot tea scorched her hands and she hurried to put the cup and saucer down on the first surface she found, a sheaf of papers to the right of Grandfather's typewriter. Fortunately, Papa C had stepped out of the office and didn't see Bertie make a saucer ring on his official correspondence. Bertie hurriedly put the cup and saucer down on the top shelf of the desk next to the kerosene light. Then she used the cotton doily next to the logbook to blot the papers with the telltale tea ring stains that now looked like someone had made sealing wax impressions several pages deep. Blaming this on Bobbie wouldn't help her, so she took the evidence of her accident to her grandmother who came up with a solution to cover the mishap.

"Bertie, the papers are too damaged to put in the post, but they are not so damaged that I can't read them well enough to re-type them. After all, I have been in charge of the weather station here for years, so I am a fair typist," she said as she sat down at the typewriter to dictate the letter to herself. "I'll start with this letter since it is an official letter to the..."

Mama Anna froze and the rest of the words of her dictation were reduced to a whisper as she barely mouthed the words *"Department of Commerce Light House Service."* Her grandmother's eyes were lit like coals that had been stoked by a fury as yet unseen before by Bertie.

Breathing deliberately and deeply, like a bellows fanning the flame of anger, Mama Anna declared, "Actually, there is no need for me to re-type *this* letter. Bertie, be a dear and go find your grandfather!"

"But Mama Anna, I'm *afraid* to tell Papa C that I've ruined his letters!"

"Not to worry, child," Mama Anna said as she rose from the typewriter and tapped the pages of the damaged letters decisively on the desk. "You only ruined a few letters. It would be another matter if you had spilled the tea on one of the official log books. Now, go and find your grandfather and tell him that I need to speak with him *immediately.* Then I want you and your brother to make yourselves scarce while your grandfather and I come to an understanding. Go where you usually go when we can't find *you.*" Bertie and Bobbie had some practice in making themselves scarce. They understood that when the inspector came to call, they were supposed to be unseen and unheard. Bertie always retreated to the staircase.

STAIRCASE

Bertie had no memory of where she had found her grandfather, but find him she had. Then she made herself scarce on her staircase balcony to listen to the unfolding drama and take refuge from her grandfather's ire over the spoiled correspondence. Bertie was spared his wrath, but her grandfather was not spared his wife's wrath over the contents of the correspondence Mama Anna held accusingly in her hands.

At first, her grandmother simply read aloud to her grandfather from the stained letter. Wisely, Bertie's grandfather didn't say a single word until she was finished.

DEPARTMENT OF COMMERCE
LIGHTHOUSE SERVICE

Eleventh District
Whitefish Point Light Station
January 5, 1918

Lighthouse Inspector,
District, Mich.

Sir:—

The season of inactivity for lightkeepers on Lake Superior is again at hand, and the thought that every man young and old should actively get behind the Government in this terrible struggle of putting down Prussianism, makes me feel as though I am not doing my share of it. Therefore, is it not possible to assign me to some duty for the winter months, or for the duration of the war for that matter? For instance, patrol duty on either land or sea. I don't care which, for I feel capable of performing either. I spent several years sailing on saltwater previous to coming to this country, so duty on water would be as agreeable as on land.

Will you not, therefore, aid me in getting into the game? I will promise to give a good account of myself if I get the chance. I have one son in training at Camp Custer, the other son has applied for enlistment and will no doubt be in it soon, so should I through your help be able to get into it, I would be the happiest man in the land, as all the man members of the family would then be doing their might to crush Kaiserism.

I am 52 years old, in good health, full of pep, and willing to go anywhere the Government sees fit to put me. I only ask, that should I get back, the station and position I am leaving be given back to me. Will you aid me to get an assignment?

Very respectfully,

Robert Carlson, Keeper

"Anna, this is lighthouse business, not *your* business," Grandfather proclaimed.

"Hur vågar du!" *How dare you!* Grandmother said in Swedish, which Bertie recalled was her default language when she was livid. "Fyren är vår verksamhet. Det har den alltid varit den kommer alltid att vara vårt... familje företag. *Lighthouse business is our business. It always has been and it always will be our business...family business.*

"What could be more *family* business than serving with my *sons*?" Robert countered.

"Våra söner och vår svärson med, för de delen, vill inte att du ska deltaga i denna konflikt. Detta är en ung mans krig." *Our sons and our son-in-law, for that matter, do not want you to serve in this conflict. This is a young man's war.* Unfortunate, but true. That's how it's always been." Anna moved closer to Robert to bridge the gap in opinion, if only physically.

"How can I sit out the war here and twiddle my thumbs when I am an able-bodied man and ready to ..."

"Vad? Offra ditt levebröd kanske till och med ditt liv." *What? Sacrifice your livelihood and, possibly, your life?* And in your proposed absence, I'm supposed to do what exactly?" Anna asked, backing up again to increase the distance between them.

"You've served as an assistant lighthouse keeper before and you can do it again, and ably, Anna," Robert said putting his hands gently on her shoulders. "Except this time, you would be the main keeper."

"That's beside the point. Of course, a woman can do anything if she sets her mind to it, but the Lighthouse Service won't let me supervise a male assistant keeper. I know that many women have become lighthouse keepers after their husbands died, but I don't intend for that to be *me.*" Anna turned and walked away to pace back and forth in the office. "So, you think it's fine for me to stay here *alone* with Bertie and Bobbie and wring my hands with constant worry for young Robert and Carl *and* you?" Anna asked as she turned back around to face Robert and pointed at him saying, "You are doing *far* more than 'twiddling your thumbs,' as you say, right here at the lighthouse," she said as she tapped her finger pointedly on his chest above his heart.

"This argument may very well be moot, because the Lighthouse Service may not give me permission," Robert said resignedly.

"You *never* should have considered asking for their *permission* before you asked for *my* opinion, let alone my blessing," Anna said putting her hand over her heart

"*If* I get permission from my *superiors, then* I'll ask for your blessing."

She moved to the window where she had kept vigil more nights than she could count. "Let me be as crystal clear as that body of water out there," Anna said pointing in the direction of the lake obscured by the dune. "I know your hearing isn't what it used to be, but you have no excuse for not listening to me. I will *never* give you my blessing and I may never *forgive* you for plotting to abandon me, our grown children, and *especially,* our young grandchildren."

"'Accusing me as having 'plotted' puts my decision in the wrong light," Robert said.

"'Plotting' or 'planning' is of no consequence at this point since this letter will never be put in the post to the Lighthouse Service," Anna said with finality.

"Anna, darling. I thought that you understood that the stained letter in your hand is only a copy."

"You mean that this letter..." Anna said accusingly as she held the paper aloft.

"I've already put the original letter in the post and now I'm waiting on an answer from the Lighthouse Service," Robert said quickly.

"Well, you already have *my* answer and you aren't likely to hear another word from me for some time!" Anna said as she turned on her heal as crisply as a soldier and left the room.

Bertie almost felt as unsettled now by the vivid memory of her grandparents' most ardent argument, as she did when she was a witness to the drama way back in January of 1918. She pitied the girl she'd once been overhearing all that. From her perch on the stairs at the back of her grandfather's office, she further pitied that innocent little girl who did not yet know that that would not be the *only* time in 1918 that the seemingly distant war would split their home apart.

"Ma'am. Are you okay? Can I help you up? Looks like you've seen a ghost." The docent, Drew, had come over to her

when she was lost in thought. "I shouldn't encourage any talk
of ghosts here at the lighthouse, should I?"

Bertie gave a wry smile. "No, I suppose not. I was
just waiting for the tour group to finish looking at the exhibit
room. I don't mean to slight the museum staff, but I'm more
interested in the domestic side of the house."

"That's okay. Tourists visit for many different reasons."
Drew turned to the tour group clustering around the bottom of
the stairs where Bertie sat.

"Shall we go upstairs to the bedrooms?" The young
man asked the others as he turned to Bertie and offered,
"After you, ma'am." Bertie would have preferred to be alone
with her memories so that she could tip-toe back into her
childhood without anyone tripping her into the present day
by calling her "ma'am" in this house where she had always
been just "Bertie." She took hold of the handrail and rose
to continue with the tour—leaving, for the time being, the
uncertainties of decades ago.

BEDROOM

Docent: *"Children of a lightkeeper lived in a world very different from that of children who lived in the cities or even small towns. Every day they were exposed to the realities of nature at Whitefish Point, the beauty of sunrises and sunsets, the drama of seasonal changes, and the harshness of the wind and the power of Lake Superior. Such a relatively isolated life meant that families were very close. Simple little things were important and had a significant impact on children's lives and they developed a special attachment to the world of their lightkeeper parents, or grandparents as would have been the case for young Bertie and Bobbie Endress. There is a door on this floor that is closed and locked, as it would have been when the Carlson family occupied this side of the residence. Other than that, feel free to look at the other bedrooms here on this floor and note the period detail in each room, from the quilts on the beds to the vintage books on the shelves that might have been used by the families stationed here."*

Bertie gazed out the window of her childhood bedroom to what used to be her private panoramic view of

Lake Superior. She had supplied the description on the wall of the seasonal views she had treasured as a child; "The fresh nights of spring, the twinkling lights of passing freighters on warm summer nights, and the cold and deadly gales of November." Just then she was rewarded by seeing a flock of snow buntings cascading chaotically past the window.

Bertie's focus returned from the distant view of the shore to the sill outside her old bedroom window where a LeConte's sparrow was perched. Bertie loved this little bird because it would sing at any time of the day and often all night long. She recalled when Reverend Law brought her the organ music for "His Eye is on the Sparrow." The lyrics were supposed to be reassuring—*"His eye is on the sparrow and I know he watches me."* But after Bertie kept an important secret from her grandparents, she thought the lyrics sounded more accusatory than comforting.

The little sparrow on the sill suddenly took flight and Bertie's attention returned to her indoor surroundings.

Bertie had been consulted about the restoration of the lighthouse keeper quarters for period detail and she had donated a few family heirlooms to lend authenticity to the effort. She was pleased with the result. However, a detail that would have lent even more authenticity to her old bedroom would have been to set a pair of child-sized shoes under the bed. Once, when the inspector's flag was spotted flying on the approaching tender ship, they all rushed around trying to pick up anything that the inspector would find amiss. However, young Bertie failed to remove her shoes from under the bed to the closet, and they were docked on the report for the infraction.

Bertie noticed that the quilts on the beds were not the ones she remembered from childhood. She had loved those quilts. Many a night, as a comforting bedtime ritual, she had traced their simple patterns with her fingers. Her favorite quilt was the one with the "tree of paradise" design, with its multi-colored triangle wedges of foliage balanced on sturdy geometric trunks. Much like life at the light, the repetitive pattern was the essence of its soothing nature. But the pattern, as beautiful as it was, still gave only the illusion of a real tree and the illusion of order. There was, after all, no lasting promise that the order of things would stay the same, even in Paradise.

Downstairs, Bertie had been preoccupied by the ghosts of the people she loved, but now when she stood in her childhood bedroom, she was haunted by the two people who hadn't lived here much—her mother and father. Sometimes, young Bertie had had trouble getting to sleep because she was so lonesome for her mother. At times, she had sought some extra attention from Mama Anna at bedtime. Bertie mused, "If these walls could talk—or whisper—they would murmur the long-ago words of comfort from Mama Anna."

"When you're scared, Mama Anna, what do you do?" Little Bertie had asked as she pulled her treasured tree quilt up to her chin.

"Well, I stay busy. If I can't *talk* myself out of being scared, then I *work* myself out of it," her grandmother had explained.

"I think talking helps me the most. Tell me a story, Mama Anna. Please?" Bertie said as she raised her head off the pillow by propping herself up with her elbows.

"What if I only know scary stories?" asked Mama Anna as she eased down to sit on the edge of the bed.

"*Don't* tell me another story about Tomte!" Bertie pleaded.

"Then how about a story about when I was scared?" Mama Anna asked, raising her eyebrows above the rim of her glasses.

"How will that help *me?*" Bertie asked incredulously.

"Well, because everything turned out fine in the end," Mama Anna said gently patting Bertie's head.

"Okay. That sounds like a good story," Anna agreed as she snuggled down again in her bed.

"So...it was our first winter at the island lighthouse in Wisconsin where your grandfather was head lighthouse keeper and his brother Carl was the assistant keeper." Mama Anna began with the hushed voice Bertie warmed to immediately.

"Did I ever live there at that lighthouse with you and Papa C?"

"No, no you didn't. Cecelia, your mama, was only about two years old and the twins, your uncles Robert and Carl, were barely 9 months old."

"So, this is really a story about how *they* got scared?" Bertie wondered.

"No. They were too little to have any inkling about what it was to be scared, and thankfully, too young to know that *I* was scared," Mama Anna chuckled lightly.

"Weren't you too *old* to get scared?" Bertie asked skeptically.

"When you get older, you're scared of different things is all," Mama Anna explained. "At any rate, one day, your grandfather and your great-uncle Carl went fishing and left me alone with the three children. I didn't even have the dogs for company because they took the dogs with them. To tell you the truth, I was always afraid to be by myself on the island. I was from Chicago and I wasn't used to such a solitary life, especially without both the lighthouse keepers around. After they left, I was so skittish that I rushed around the house locking all the doors and windows."

"Did you hear a noise outside?" Bertie asked while looking nervously toward her window at the gloomy darkness outside.

"Just the same wind I always heard, but it sounded more and more menacing to me as the day wore on. Finally, it was so dark outside, that I didn't want to look out the window, but I had to keep watching for the men. I paced between peering out the window and sitting by the fire trying to thaw my fear."

"Were they late in returning?" Bertie asked, wriggling down deeper under the quilt.

"They were supposed to return by dinnertime that night, but they didn't. I sat up all night waiting and watching. By the morning, I was in such an anxious state. Then, I realized that I had to milk the cow for the children, but I had never milked the cow and I was afraid of her. She could really kick. I went down to the barn and looked at the cow.

She swung her head toward me and made a noise that did nothing to quell my fears and I knew I could never milk her as I had seen your grandfather do. Running into the woodshed, I grabbed the axe, and in desperation began chopping at the wall of the cow's stall. I hacked away at the wall until I had a hole through which I could put both hands. Then I started to milk into a little tin cup, which I held with one hand, while I milked the cow with the other. The cow kicked and I jumped away, but I had to keep at it for the children's sake." Mama Anna described the whole scene as if it were happening before her very eyes.

"But you were still all alone?" Bertie asked.

"Yes, except for the babies and your mother, for a few more anguish-filled days. When I could get the three little ones to sleep for the night, I would go down to the shore to continue my vigil and beckon the men back to the island by wishing the harsh wind would blow them back to me," Mama Anna said as she shivered and folded her arms around her like a shawl.

"Did you try praying for their return?

"If you call screaming into the wind praying, then I believe so!" Mama Anna laughed out loud. She went on to explain more about the conditions on the island. "You don't know what the Michigan Island shore is, in winter. Unbroken trails through the woods, ice hummocks barring the way, deep gulches of snow into which I stumbled, the bitter, cutting wind from the lake lashing my face. And above all, the sight of that white expanse that was holding my husband from me."

"I can't picture you screaming into the wind." Bertie shook her head in disbelief.

"Sometimes, when we think we can't endure any longer, it does us good to let go like that. I think if I had not screamed, I would have lost my mind," Mama Anna said with conviction.

"How long were you on your own?" Bertie asked sleepily as she turned on her side.

Mama Anna stroked Bertie's arm as she answered, "The men finally returned, but not until the eve of the third night. They didn't mean to stay away so long, but the ice had broken up while the men were fishing and the platform of ice that they were on was carried out into the open lake."

"How did Grandfather and Great Uncle Carl get back to shore?" Bertie asked with the slightly slurred speech of drifting off to sleep.

"That's a story you'll have to get your grandfather to tell you about on another night." Mama Anna then tucked Bertie in and put her hand lightly on her brow. "I don't know why we feel frightened sometimes here in this place where we should feel the safest. Of all people, we should feel the very safest in a lighthouse because that's what our home is—a light in the darkest and most treacherous of nights."

Bertie rallied as she tried to stay awake. "And we're never really alone because we have neighbors just on the other side of the wall. Sometimes, I wish I could see the other side of the lighthouse, as if their half were my dollhouse and I could watch them and maybe even change the furniture all around."

Mama Anna laughed. "If you're having thoughts about spying on our neighbors, then I need to ask your grandfather to build you a dollhouse of your very own. Sometimes I get curious about the Schroeders, too, but we have the best of both worlds here."

"What do you mean?" Bertie asked as she started to dream about having a dollhouse.

"They're close by if we need them, but we don't get in each other's business. Or at least," Mama Anna said almost under her breath, "I don't think we do."

LOCKED DOOR AND LONG AGO

Bertie felt a sudden urge to put her ear to the door that led to the other half of the lighthouse just like she did as a little girl when no one was watching. She hadn't ever understood the words she overheard from the "dollhouse" side of the lighthouse. She wondered if they also eavesdropped from their side. They might have heard her daily argument with her grandmother about practicing the organ. However, Reverend Law, the "Sky Pilot," had helped to smooth their feathers when he brought Bertie the gift of a book of hymns. He remembered about her love of birds and had put a bookmark in the page for "His Eye is on the Sparrow."

Bertie could scarcely forget that they shared the lighthouse with another family because she and Bobbie were so often "shushed" by their grandparents when they got too boisterous indoors. The Schroeders didn't have children. Other children would have made welcome playmates. Her grandmother also would have welcomed having a friend next door. Bertie once overheard her grandmother remark to Papa C that the assistant lighthouse keeper might as well be single for all the interaction she had with his wife. Occasionally, on baking day. Mama Anna had shared with the Schroeders some Swedish dishes, like kroppkaka potato dumplings and kladdkaka cake, but her gestures were never reciprocated. That both puzzled and irked Mama Anna. Yet, even Papa C complained himself soon afterward about Mr. Schroeder's habit of not storing the lighthouse tools properly in the tool shed. He continually worried about the surprise inspections required by the U.S. Lighthouse Service. The loss of a tool simply could not be tolerated. Even a used paintbrush had to be turned in and would not be replaced until the bristles were worn down to the metal ferrule. Carlson's most recent inventory of tools revealed a missing wrench and this really concerned him.

Docent: *"As you can see there is nothing remarkable about this hallway. There is a door to the assistant lightkeeper's residence and a door to the jointly accessed covered bridge to the tower. We do, however, need to pause here to wait for the tour group ahead of us to come back down from seeing the lighthouse lantern and enjoying the view from there, which is eighty feet above Lake Superior. While we wait, I wonder if anyone has a question?"*

"I was fascinated," said a man sporting a veteran's ball cap, "to read on the exhibit sign about the espionage plot uncovered here in 1918. I think that was the year. Can you elaborate on that?"

Docent: *"Certainly. Many people want to know if the story about the German spies here at the light is true. There actually was a WWI era plan called 'Operation Snow Owl' hatched by the Germans to disrupt the shipping of iron ore in the Great Lakes as it was being transported through what the Germans referred to as "pinch-points," like the Soo Locks. The goal was to cripple the manufacture of munitions for the war effort.*

However, we can only be confident of the facts surrounding the incident in question at Whitefish Point. They go as follows: 1918 was a time of high anti-German sentiment throughout the US. Robert Carlson's two sons were fighting against the Germans so he might not have been too keen to have a German immigrant as an assistant keeper. Also, it was said that Carlson was not easy to get along with, so it was possible that there was a conflict between the two keepers for one reason or another. There is a book entitled "Remotely Yours" that mentions something about the assistant keeper throwing a wrench at Carlson when he was in the tool shed. This supposed attack and Carlson's subsequent discovery that the assistant lightkeeper wasn't replenishing the fuel to operate the light on his shift, apparently led Carlson to discreetly call the inspector whereby help then arrived promptly by water and Schroeder was arrested.

However, we have a problem confirming that Schroder was an actual spy because we have only one source for this story—the memory of an 8-year-old girl, Bertie Endress, the lighthouse keeper's young granddaughter. Maybe we shouldn't perpetuate a story that might be more legend than legitimate history. It's popularly regarded as historical, but since it hasn't been authenticated and might be unreliable information, we should probably remove any reference to this story here at the lighthouse. However, if you didn't get to read the sign about the supposed espionage plot, I don't mind repeating the quote. At least this story is much more interesting than the ghost stories that proliferate about lighthouses."

"Excuse me. May I recite the quote about the whole matter from the sign that's here at the museum?" Bertie interjected.

"Sure?" Drew answered skeptically. "But the sign is mounted on the wall of the bedroom around the corner."

"Not a problem. I've got the gist of it because I was that 'unreliable' 8-year-old girl," Bertie said pointedly.

When Bertie revealed her identity, the tour group murmured and immediately moved to give her center stage— as much as was possible in cramped quarters.

Bertie continued, "It was on a seemingly ordinary July day in 1918. Suddenly, my younger brother and I were not let out of the house and a government boat with men I had never seen before appeared. Furniture was taken from the assistant lightkeeper's house and the assistant and his wife were removed in handcuffs. The assistant was sullenly silent, but his wife was screaming and cursing in English and German. It seems that the Schroeders had been sent by the German government to disrupt shipping by putting the light and fog signal out of commission. I clearly remember standing at the window upstairs with my grandmother and my mother, as we watched the couple being taken away."

"You'll have to forgive me, ma'am, I wasn't told that you were going to be on my tour this morning," Drew exclaimed as his complexion flushed to the roots of his curly dark hair. "Folks, this is a bit of a surprise. May I?" he cautiously inquired of Bertie, and she nodded her assent.

"Thank you. Allow me to introduce Bertie Endress Rollo, the Carlson's granddaughter we've been learning a bit about this morning. Tomorrow this very building will be dedicated to her. It is an honor to have you with us," Drew graciously offered, even though he was clearly a bit unnerved, and understandably so with this sudden revelation that he had been standing in as an expert on the Carlsons in front of a member of that very family.

"It would be great to interview you later, if you have time, that is," Drew said trying to gain his equilibrium. "Would you leave me a note with one of the cashiers at the gift shop about when and where we could meet later today, if that's alright?" Drew asked.

"Thank you, young man, that would be nice. And may I thank all of you for having an interest in the life of lighthouse keepers and their families," Bertie said, taking a step back and giving all indication that she was dropping back into silence and returning the small stage, as it were, to the young docent.

"You might think that it is reasonable to doubt the recollection of an 8-year-old girl." Bertie stepped back into the spotlight, clearly surprising both Drew and the visitors that she was going to continue. She did, however, have the complete, even rapt attention of all. "You might have further reason to doubt her, that is, my childhood account, because I was just 'one source,' the only source it seems, for this story, but my mother and grandmother were there, too, and we all saw the same thing. Thereafter, we talked about it many times over the years. That day was also significant for me in another respect because my mother was seldom at the lighthouse, so when she was, those times were and remain especially memorable for me."

"Living at the lighthouse was wonderful, but it was, I admit, very monotonous. That's why moments that were out of the ordinary, like the arrest of the Schroeders, really stood out. I was raised by lighthouse keepers who kept daily logbooks on everything from the weather to the bodies that sometimes washed ashore. My grandparents set an example by having me keep a daily log or diary of my activities as a kind of schooling, really. I developed a lifelong habit of recording and reflecting on my days. Young man, in one of my diaries, I have a contemporaneous account of that same day in 1918."

"Thank you for your added insights, Mrs. Rollo. I'm still a little embarrassed that I was unaware that you were on the tour," Drew said as his blush was abating.

"Please. Call me Bertie. And I'm a little embarrassed, too, that I have taken over your tour and you were doing such a good job. I may have spoken out of turn. I had no intention of doing that today. Really, I had intended to blend in with the wallpaper."

"It's not a problem at all. Would you like to share more about your experiences living here at the light as we move on to the tour of the tower?" Drew asked sincerely.

"I'd be happy to do that if only I had not become so afraid of heights over the years, which is one of the many reasons that I didn't take up the family business of lighthouse keeping," Bertie said while noting that the tour group enjoyed the irony of her revelation. "I'll just let myself out. After all, I know the way."

LIGHTHOUSE TOWER

Bertie felt a little awkward about having upstaged Drew, but maybe she could make it up to him by treating him to an early dinner with her at the Little Falls Inn restaurant just down the road. He seemed sincerely interested in learning more details about life at the light, so she would leave a message at the gift shop counter for him. She suspected Drew might be as hungry for more information as he would be for a free meal.

While Bertie descended the stairs to part ways with the tour group, she did so with a bit of a heavy step. Her *thoughts,* however, were ascending more lightly up the tower stairs. The ones she had traveled so often as a little girl with her grandfather. Bertie had thought that the ironwork of the stairsteps to the lantern was beautiful, especially seen from above because each step looked like the staves of a black lace fan. In her imagination, the iron filigree "fans" kept the flame for the Fresnel lens going in between the lightkeepers' shifts. The light was a kerosene mantle light floating on a bed of mercury. Each night, on every watch, the light had to be wound up. Weights slipped on a rope that extended from the light base to within a foot off the ground in a special pipe or tower of its own. When cranked up with a handle, the weights rose. It was the slow descent of the weights that caused the lights to turn. Bertie could still hear the whispered whoosh of the big flare when her grandfather lit the mantle and the torch, like a baton, was handed over to the life-saving flame fueling the Whitefish Point beacon.

When Bertie reached the bottom of the stairs, she was once again in her grandfather's office. She took a few minutes to pause there and with her hand still on the newel post of the railing, she gazed appreciatively at her "grandfather's" back, intent on his task at his desk. Bertie had always been curious about her grandfather's roll-top desk with its many drawers and doors, nooks and niches, that concealed the contents like the compartments of an advent calendar. As she had longed to do as a child, she wanted to reach around the seated figure to explore the pigeonholes of the desk. The mannequin sentinel seemed almost as imposing as her grandfather had been, especially while he was composing correspondence on his "Smith and Sons" typewriter with the rhythmic drive of a Bach toccata—each phrase punctuated by the clarion bell of the carriage.

She marveled at what a fortuitous decision it was, on the part of the Lighthouse Board, to reject her grandfather's request to serve on active duty during WWI. Her grandfather's superiors had deemed that Robert Carlson's job at the Whitefish light was too important itself to the war effort. In fact, the Board saw it as an "essential service," so much so that granting him the leave he requested was out of the question. How very prescient that decision turned out to be when the war was brought right to their doorstep—right to the stairsteps of the lighthouse tower—insidiously trodden upon by a German spy. Yet there was keeper Carlson, on duty, serving on the front lines to protect and defend the northern Michigan coastline...and the Carlson family...and the country.

Of course, Bertie had not taken the "oath of office" like her grandfather had. Still, it was an unwritten understanding that the whole family—Mama Anna, Bertie, and Bobbie—were also entrusted with the duties and defense associated with living at the light. However, it hadn't always been clear to young Bertie as to what that meant exactly. Bertie looked at her grandfather's stand-in at the desk and thought about how she might apologize to him for breaking the family vow through her childhood indiscretion.

Bertie had wanted Bobbie, a retired minister, to come to the dedication weekend and give the benediction, but a recent hip surgery kept him from traveling. Bertie understood, as she mused that Bobbie, of course, was no longer as spry as that poseable mannequin in the lighthouse residence.

Bertie never would have guessed that her brother Bobbie would become a minister. While growing up at the light together, Bertie and Bobbie endured long stretches of solitude that gave rise to a good deal of squabbling between them. It amused Bertie to think that their childhood just might have been the perfect preparation for a minister's life of contemplation and counseling. In all likelihood the true inspiration for Bobbie's career was the influence of Reverend Law's visits. He always had time to talk to Bobbie and Bertie, and he had the patience to entertain all the questions Bobbie peppered him with on a variety of subjects. Reverend Law had more patience than Papa C often did with Bobbie's inquisitive nature.

Over the years, Bertie noticed that her brother had turned his rambunctious and relentlessly chatty character inside out in adulthood becoming a most sympathetic listener for other people's questions, concerns, and needs. Bertie had counted on Bobbie's understanding nature when she decided to unburden herself of a secret from her childhood that decades earlier had cast a shadow on her memories of living at the light. She hadn't aired any painful memories in her memoir, which she had initially referred to as "my little book." Still, the local historian who compiled her stories insisted on calling it her memoir. Bertie didn't think it qualified for such a pretentious label, especially since she didn't reveal any deep dark secrets. Yet, the interest in her memoir and her help with the restoration of the keepers' residence had dredged up the mental debris from a storm in which she had found herself in the eye of as a child and the painful memory of that time that kept washing ashore in her subconscious.

So, one day, the month before the dedication, Bertie decided to confide in Bobbie, even though she would have to do so over the phone. She had called him a week earlier intending to discuss the Schroeder incident, but lacked the courage to do anything more than chat about her donation to the museum. Now with her renewed resolve, she gripped the receiver and she settled in for a proper chat at her breakfast nook with a cup of Söderblandning tea and a view of her birdfeeder. The tea was too hot to sip, but she "drank" in the aroma—a mix of birch and berries. With a sigh of resignation and relief, she was finally ready to make the call.

After just a couple of rings, Bobbie picked up. After a few of the usual questions and pleasantries, Bertie prefaced her revelation by telling Bobbie she had a difficult and decades-long secret that threatened to sink her more pleasant thoughts about returning to their childhood home for the dedication.

"Do you need me to listen to you as a brother or as a minister?" Bobbie asked gently, as he put aside his crossword puzzle.

"Both, I suppose?" Bertie answered tentatively, as she lifted the teacup to take a cautious sip.

"I don't necessarily encourage people to confess things to me, but talking about one's problems can act as 'mental first aid' as Reverend Law used to say," Bobbie offered as he lightly tapped his temple.

"I had forgotten that he used to talk about his mission in that way." The memory elicited a smile from Bertie.

"You aren't about to admit that you stole a book from one of his library crates, are you?" Bobbie teased.

"If only my indiscretion were so trivial, Bobbie. That's why I don't know where to start." Bertie put her hands around the cup for the comforting warmth.

"Bertie, I'm assuming you're talking about a childhood mistake?" Bobbie reached across his kitchen table for something to take notes on, if necessary. This was a ministerial habit he had developed to wade through a parishioner's story for the most pertinent information.

"Yes. But I've thought of what I did so many times in my adulthood, I feel almost like I committed this crime as an adult," Bertie admitted as she fiddled nervously with the telephone cord.

"Bertie, I'm sure you are being much too hard on yourself. Take me back to the time of this childhood memory and maybe I'll remember something that would help give you some perspective," Bobbie offered.

"That would be more than I could expect…more than I deserve," Bertie sighed as she watched a Chipping sparrow at her feeder.

"Let's try," Bobbie urged her.

"Do you remember being invited over to the Schroeder's side of the lighthouse to make a gingerbread house?"

"I sure do! And I also remember how Mama Anna thought it was a waste of the flour that the tender ships brought to us to make something so frivolous."

Bertie mulled over the memory of how frugal their grandparents were—or had to be. "She was probably right, but we were so in need of entertainment that we were eager to go over to the other side to visit, even though there were no children. Remember how Mrs. Schroeder had sketched the lighthouse and had baked all the different shapes to recreate the exterior of our divided home?" Bertie asked.

"Yes, that, too, but I'm amazed that I haven't thought about that visit in years, probably not since then. I do remember that it was great fun to put the gingerbread pieces together. The frosting was flavored with maple syrup, as I recall," Bobbie said reflexively licking his lips.

"And there were several times that the gingerbread house split apart and we giggled with Mrs. Schroeder about the collapse," Bertie said, the pace of her words picking up with the clarity of the recollection aided by sharing a common memory with her brother.

"Yes, that was fun. But, Bertie, I don't remember anything that happened that day—anything that you did—that would cause you concern today."

"I set events in motion that day by asking Mr. Schroeder something. I asked him to build me a lighthouse that wouldn't fall apart—a dollhouse version of our lighthouse with two sides open to the outside so I could play with the dolls and furniture on both sides. I knew that he was good at building miniature things because of the Christmas pyramid he made for me for my birthday."

"I remember that gift. All I got was a harmonica," Bobbie said pretending to be aggrieved. "The Schroeders did seem to prefer you, as I recall. Is that what you've felt guilty about all these years?"

"No. To be honest, I selfishly enjoyed the attention of Mrs. Schroeder, especially. I wonder if I made her into a stand-in for our mother. Mrs. Schroeder was childless, and in some ways, we were sometimes motherless. But, as we all found out about six months later, the Schroeders might as well have been figures in a dollhouse because there wasn't anything genuine about them," Bertie said with the dull sting of long-ago regret.

"You can't blame yourself for not knowing that they were spies. Since you were older than I was, you probably felt the pain of their betrayal more than I did," Bobbie offered.

"Probably. But once I had asked for the dollhouse, that request touched off events like the collapsing walls of our gingerbread house."

"How so, Bertie?" Bobbie asked in cautious disbelief.

"One day when I was visiting the Schroeders, Mrs. Schroeder was fussing over me by fixing my hair in braids and coiling them like a crown on my head. I enjoyed the motherly attention, but when I came back over to our side of the lighthouse, Mama Anna was annoyed because she had already fixed my hair in ringlets and then Mrs. Schroeder had made it look like I had, according to Mama Anna, 'a breadbasket on my head.'" Bertie touched her thinning puff of hair wistfully.

"I remember that day. Papa C said you looked nice and Mama Anna gave him a frosty glare. You stomped up the stairs to your room and left me downstairs—invisible in the wake of your anger—to listen in on Mama Anna and Papa C's conversation. Mama Anna was angry that Mrs. Schroeder was treating you like a life-size doll. She was worried that you were getting too attached to her because you needed a mother."

"She wasn't wrong. That was just another betrayal of my family." Bertie shifted in her chair.

Bobbie continued, "Papa C said that our mother was getting better and might be home by summer. And he reminded Mama Anna that assistant lighthouse keepers did tend to move on with some regularity for one reason or another. Anyway, that argument wasn't your fault, Bertie. Our grandparents argued from time to time, and they probably argued more often about me."

"Yes, but your hijinks were nothing compared to what I did," Bertie insisted.

"What *did* you do?" Bobbie asked with keen interest.

"Mrs. Schroeder told me that her husband wanted to make my dollhouse as realistic as possible to surprise our grandparents. She said it might even be valuable someday as a family heirloom. I didn't care anything about a family heirloom, but I did want to surprise our grandparents," Bertie said and then paused to take a sip of the cooled tea.

"So, you kept the *dollhouse* a secret?" Bobbie said as he tried to lead the conversation to the point of the alleged transgression.

"That's not it. You see, Mrs. Schroeder asked me to leave the door upstairs unlocked to our half of the lighthouse when we went to church one day so that she and her husband could go take a look at all the rooms to jot down the dimensions to make sketches of the rooms and their furnishings. And I did it. Later, after the Schroeders had been arrested and we went in their side of the lighthouse, there wasn't any half-made dollhouse, of course." Bertie grimaced with the memory of how disillusioned she had felt by the discovery.

"*Now* I understand," Bobbie said with a validating tsk that signaled his new insight into his sister's mindset. "It *was* a breach of security, of course, to allow them access to the head lighthouse keeper's house, his office, and records."

"I've never been able to forgive myself for that lapse in judgment all those years ago," Bertie said taking a deep breath to counteract how deflated she felt with these revelations.

"However, it wasn't a lapse in judgment when you were too young to know the implications, Bertie. You were an unwitting pawn in an adult game—an international game of espionage. If you ask *me*, the Lighthouse Board was at fault for not properly vetting the Schroeders," Bobbie said with conviction.

"I should have told you this years ago," Bertie sighed as she felt some of the guilt begin to ebb away.

"I wish you had, Bertie. It's just possible, though, that your actions *may* have hastened the events that led to the Schroeder's arrest *before* they could do any real harm to us or to the country."

Bertie chewed her bottom lip briefly before she could admit, "I *guess* that could be possible."

"And remember. Grandfather's, shall we say, irrational plan to leave his post to serve in combat *truly* would have been inviting the fox into the henhouse. And on that score, I have something to admit to *you*, Bertie."

"Oh?"

"For years I thought your memory of the Schroeder's arrest wasn't," Bobbie hesitated, and then said, "true."

"Bobbie, how could you think that I would lie?" Bertie asked, wounded.

"I didn't think that you would lie, Bertie. I thought you trusted your childhood memory a bit too much. To me that spy story was just too outlandish to be believed. However, when you told me a few months ago that there was going to be a dedication event at Whitefish Point, I suspected that you would be asked about the Germans, so I did a little research to find some sort of corroborating evidence for the possible positioning of spies at Whitefish Point and the strategic importance of Michigan in WWI."

"And?" Bertie asked hopefully.

"I found the information in an article in a Detroit magazine entitled something like 'The Spies All Around Us,' I think."

"Was it about the Schroeders?" Bertie asked with mixed feelings because it still hurt to think about how they had duped her into trusting them.

"No, it wasn't about *your* spies."

"*My* spies!" Bertie countered but she knew that they *were* 'hers' in that she was the person in the family who was the most taken with the Schroeders—the one who was most affected by their presence and even more affected by their exit in handcuffs. In fact, she felt so guilty, she'd left the whole incident out of her memoir.

"Sorry, Bertie. It wasn't about the spies among us at Whitefish Point. Oh, I remember the article title now—"The Spies Among Us!" The article focused on a German spy named 'K' something. I could try to remember the details of the story, but it would be easier if I read it to you. Let me look. I have a pile of papers here on the kitchen counter." Bertie heard Bobbie shuffling through his papers, the sound of which mimicked how he had ruffled her feathers emotionally by disclosing his skepticism about her childhood memory.

"Here it is!" Bobbie announced as he began to read aloud from the article.

"'In 1915, Detroit was the target of a plot to blow up local manufacturing companies, such as the Detroit Screw Works, that was manufacturing shrapnel for the Allied troops. German immigrant and Detroit resident Albert Kaltschmidt was busy buying dynamite, cutting it into small pieces, painting it black, and tossing it surreptitiously into the coal bunkers of vessels in the Detroit River. In May 1915, Kaltschmidt met with several German immigrants in the Kresge Building. He told those assembled that their duty lay in the destruction of munitions destined for the Allies in Europe and asked for their help in blowing up a factory in Detroit, according to *The Historical Dictionary of World War I Intelligence* by Nigel West. Kaltschmidt furnished the men with suitcases full of dynamite. Another plan was to send an explosive-laden 'devil car' ingeniously coasting on roller skates into the Port Huron tunnel.

The money Kaltschmidt used to buy the dynamite and to pay the saboteurs came from Count Johann von Bernstorff, the German ambassador in Washington, D.C., and Captain Franz von Papen, who later became Adolf Hitler's vice chancellor. US authorities had been keeping an eye on the gang for some time. So, it didn't take long for Kaltschmidt and five others to be indicted. Kaltschmidt was charged with conspiring to destroy the Detroit Screw Works and that he conspired to blow up the Grand Trunk tunnel at Port Huron, one of the skates being produced as evidence in the 1917 trial against Kaltschmidt and his co-defendants.

The trial began on December 6, 1917, before federal Judge Arthur J. Tuttle, according to the United States District Court for the Eastern District of Michigan. The trial dominated newspaper coverage. On Dec. 22, 1917, the jury, after deliberating for 14 hours, convicted all but one defendant. Kaltschmidt was sentenced to four years in the U.S. Penitentiary at Leavenworth, Kansas, and fined $20,000. He served only three years, to the disgust of Judge Tuttle, and was deported soon after.'"

"That's certainly a lot of information to take in. The main thing is that you believe me now, don't you?" Bertie asked Bobbie.

"Well, this information *does* put the Schroeders' spy activities into a larger context."

"And?" Bertie gently pleaded.

"I believe you, Bertie," conceded Bobbie, "and I also believe, with even more conviction, that you shouldn't feel guilty for any part you think you played in allowing the Schroeders access to our side of the lighthouse. It's completely understandable what you did. Consider this, if you will. The *real* culprit was the heavy sense of longing that comes with lighthouse life. Only people who have lived at a lighthouse, like the two of us, can understand the cost that longing exacts."

Bertie nodded her head in silent acknowledgment of the true communion of experience that only siblings share.

Bobbie continued with what Bertie recognized as a tone he used from the pulpit. "I want you to forgive the little girl you were, Bertie. It's only fair to 'her' *then* and it's only fair to you *now*. I want you to move ahead with a clear conscience and compassion for yourself. Okay?"

"I will." Bertie sniffed as she took off her glasses to dab the tears that her brother's empathetic response had elicited. He had tapped into her reservoir of regret and released the floodgates. Bertie was so grateful for the perspective that Bobbie had offered her as her brother and as a minister, especially coming a few weeks before she would return to Whitefish Point.

Now, finishing up the lighthouse tour, she still wanted to set the record straight about a few things about the spy incident, so she was even more eager to meet with Drew over dinner. Yet, she was determined not to divulge her private shame about what role she might have played as a child in the espionage scenario, even though it would serve to underline the truth of her account. She merely wanted to set the record straight about the Schroeders and set the record straight as well about both her grandparent's contributions to defending the coast.

LITTLE FALLS INN RESTAURANT
PARADISE, MICHIGAN
SEPTEMBER 13, 1996

Before Bertie exited the lighthouse, she decided to go against the pattern for tour traffic and visit the kitchen once more. She wanted to say goodbye to "Mama Anna." Bertie was glad that the mannequin was positioned in front of the window so that the figure was backlit obscuring Bertie's view which hid how unlifelike the facial features of the figure actually were.

Unfortunately, the domestic tableau would leave visitors on the tour with the impression that her grandmother's contributions to the lighthouse were confined to the kitchen. Drew's presentation also gave short shrift to her grandmother's role in the functioning of the lighthouse. She would hope to address that oversight if he had the time to meet her for dinner. Bertie would be certain to leave a note for Drew with the cashiers in the gift shop. Even though she looked forward to the possibility of dinner with Drew, she was reluctant to leave the lighthouse.

Just before Bertie left the kitchen for the back door, she glanced at the hand pump at the kitchen sink and realized how thirsty she was, especially for the crystalline taste of the water that had spilled from that spout. Since using the pump was well beyond her daring, Bertie would have to wait to quench her thirst over dinner.

It was difficult to decide to leave the lighthouse. However, she knew that she would return, not only tomorrow but in the future. The familiar saying, "You can't go home again" rang true for Bertie in many ways, but she *could* go home again, thanks to the Shipwreck Historical Society and her vivid memories.

Now that thirst *and* hunger were calling Bertie away from the light station, she went directly to the gift shop and left a note for Drew at the counter inviting him to meet her at the "Little Falls Inn Restaurant." She was motivated to return to her car—with just a glance back to the lighthouse— and make the short trip down the road to the restaurant in Paradise to wait for dinner and Drew.

Before long Bertie was seated at a table in the restaurant. She took a quick look at the menu and then she immersed herself in making a few notes about what more she might have time to share with Drew about living at the lighthouse. Top of mind was her grandparents' contributions as lighthouse keepers, and the veracity of her childhood observations of the German spies. She usually thought of them as "the Schroeders," instead of "the spies" because she still preferred to think of the couple that she knew *before* the arrest—the people who *acted* like an aunt and uncle—when no relatives lived closer than Chicago.

Several minutes later, Drew still hadn't appeared, so Bertie, resignedly, used the time to write a postcard to a cousin on her grandmother's side still living in Chicago. Bertie had purchased the cards at the gift shop, but she hadn't selected any of the cards with images of shipwrecks because they didn't hold any appeal for her. Maritime tragedies hit too close to home for members of a lighthouse-keeping family. She didn't understand the fascination some people had for these catastrophic events.

"Hello, ma'am," said Drew.

"Well, here you are!" Bertie greeted. "For a second, I thought you were the waiter."

"Would you mind if we ordered and then talk while we eat?"

"Of course. Let's do that. I had time to decide what I wanted to order," Bertie said as she summoned the waitress.

"I would like a beef pastie and don't spare the gravy. And ice water, please," she said, watching the young woman write it on her pad.

"And I'll have the whitefish po'boy and a Two-Hearted ale. Thanks."

They handed back the menus to the waitress with the thick-as-pastie-gravy Yooper accent and Bertie was struck by the difference in Michigander accents across the state. She then addressed Drew. "I gathered you're not from around here. That is, I don't detect anything like our waitress' accent."

"I grew up in Calumet, but I went to Michigan, down state, where I guess I lost much of my accent," Drew explained.

"You obviously know where I grew up, but, like you, I can dial up or dial down my accent, at will. Tomorrow at the dedication ceremony, I may just 'dial up' my UP accent," Bertie said with a wink. "Like you, I may have 'dialed down' my UP accent when I attended the University of Michigan."

"What degree did you earn?"

"Well, I didn't. I had to withdraw because I became ill and never returned to finish."

"Oh," Drew said with an expression of genuine regret for her. "I'm sorry to hear that."

"Things happen," Bertie responded in grateful acknowledgment of Drew's sincerity. She didn't add that having rheumatic fever caused her to be bedridden for three years. However, it was a time that wasn't entirely unproductive. She spent hours upon hours watching, really studying, the birds that came to the birdfeeder just outside her window. She learned about many more birds with the help of her *Peterson's Field Guide*. Her reading of that guide was like a daily devotional that offered hope for a coming time when she might go birding outside again and be as free to come and go as they did. To change the subject Bertie asked Drew, "How did you come to be an intern at the Shipwreck Museum?"

"My mother got me interested in lighthouses because she has been a long-time member of the preservation group that works to maintain the Eagle Harbor lighthouse near Calumet."

"Have you heard of Mary Wheatley, the lady lighthouse keeper who tended the Eagle Harbor light about a hundred years ago?" Bertie asked.

"Yes, I have. She served from 1898 to 1905," Drew answered like a docent of that lighthouse, too, without the slightest hesitation in producing the exact dates of Wheatley's service.

"I'm not a historian, of course, but I'm a bit of a history buff when it comes to women who were formally appointed by the U.S. Light House Service, like my grandmother, or were *informally* serving at light stations, also like my grandmother."

"I seem to recall that Mary Wheatley's husband was also a lighthouse keeper," Drew added.

"Yes. Her husband James served at the Granite Island lighthouse as the assistant keeper while their son William was the head keeper. There were often several lighthouse keepers in one family. Tragically, William drowned in a storm coming back to Granite Island in 1898. His father was then appointed to head keeper at the Granite Island lighthouse."

"Hmm. The year of the son's drowning coincides with the date that Mary Wheatley became the keeper at Eagle Harbor," Drew stated.

"Yes, the year coincides, but that was no coincidence."

"Your evidence for that is...?"

"Just that it was unusual, if not unprecedented, that a married couple served as lightkeepers at two different lights at the same time," Bertie said.

"Maybe they just needed the dual incomes?" Drew suggested.

"That's a reasonable explanation," Bertie admitted, "but I think there's a more likely reason the couple lived apart."

"Oh, what would that be?"

"I think that it's entirely possible that the two might not have been able to support one another in their shared grief. What I mean is, Mary Wheatley may not have *sought* to distance herself from her grieving husband, but when she was given the *opportunity* to serve at a different lighthouse, she may have seized on the chance. She may have needed to grieve for her son—alone—at the Eagle Harbor light," Bertie concluded.

"You obviously know a good bit more about them than I do, but is there any evidence for that theory?" Drew asked.

"I think of those dates as bookends. The *real* story *can* be found by contemplating the human story between historical dates. I'm interested in *that* kind of history," Bertie asserted.

"Is that really history or is it more the stuff of novels?" Drew questioned.

"Or, perhaps, something in between, like memoirs," Bertie offered.

"I actually learned in one of my history classes that even memoirs aren't always reliable sources of information," Drew advanced.

That certainly wasn't Bertie's perspective. Her memoir was considered credible enough for the Great Lakes Shipwreck Historical Society to use as source material for the renovation of the lighthouse residence. After all, that's one of the reasons why the house museum was going to be dedicated to her. Unfortunately, Bertie realized she and Drew were back at square one with Drew's skepticism about her having witnessed the arrest of the German spies all those years ago. What he might not be able to comprehend was that the experience of seeing the couple who were dear to her little girl's heart arrested and pulled away from the light station and her affections was traumatic and, therefore, it was seared into her memory. She declined to give voice to these thoughts, however.

"I brought a small tape recorder," Drew said somewhat jarring Bertie out of her thoughts. "Would you mind if I use it while we talk, so I can remember anything that I might want to add to my docent notes? The restaurant isn't all that crowded, so it wouldn't be too noisy to make a decent recording." Drew's hand hovered over the recorder waiting hopefully for Bertie's permission.

"I suppose it would be alright, but then I'll feel like everything I say has to be so important," Bertie said as she grimaced a bit.

"Why don't you tell me the first thing that pops into your head—just as a warm-up—so you can get comfortable

with being recorded?" Drew asked as he moved the recorder
on the table a little closer to Bertie.

"Well, before you got here, I was looking at the menu,
and I was reminded of an anecdote about what was 'on
the menu' during thin times at the lighthouse," Bertie said,
warming to the idea of a recorded interview.

"That sounds good. Why don't you start there?"
Drew encouraged.

Taking a sip of her ice water, Bertie began, "The
Clover—our government supply boat—had brought our winter
groceries on her final run before winter freeze-up and we
thought we were all set when we received several men to
go over the fog signal and do repairs. After they left, men
from the Sault camp came up to ice fish and of course, we
fed them too. Winter came early and stayed late. The snow
was heavy and the ice was thick. Our supplies dwindled.
Deer were scarce to none. Finally, my grandfather went out
and set traps for us. Day after day until the middle of May
we had rabbit twice a day. We felt our ears grow long and
our noses beginning to twitch. We didn't walk—we hopped!
Bread became scarce as our flour, too, went down. Crackers
became a substitute for bread. Daily we looked for the
icebreakers, but we failed to see their smoke. The ice was
so thick you couldn't fish. Finally, we saw the *Wawatam*—
she was used as an icebreaker deluxe—leading a flock
of icebreakers followed by the *Clover* with our food and
supplies of all kinds. My grandmother was so glad she cried
and Bobbie and I danced and cheered. My grandfather broke
his snares before he went to the fog signal. From that day to
this none of us has eaten rabbit!"

"Stories like this are why you are going to be flooded with questions at the lighthouse dedication tomorrow," Drew said, "*and* you'll bring your grandparents alive for the attendees."

"About that. I'm particularly interested in shining a light on my *grandmother's* contributions to the station, that is, beyond her gift for stretching the food rations to include feeding more than just our family, especially during the 'Meatless Tuesdays' and 'Wheatless Wednesdays' of WWI."

"Of course," Drew encouraged. "Please don't let your dinner get cold," Drew urged. "I'll give you a moment while I get out my notebook to make some contemporaneous notes, too."

After a few minutes of savoring the taste of her pastie meat pie, the Finnish comfort food of the Upper Peninsula, Bertie was eager to continue. "My grandmother tripled herself with all the roles she filled. Wives of keepers were often officially named as assistant keepers. My grandmother was even farmed out, as she referred to the time she served as an acting assistant for nine days in 1905 at the Granite Island, Michigan lighthouse following the drowning death of the assistant keeper. Later, my grandmother was named the acting assistant keeper at the Marquette Station with my grandfather. She didn't officially serve as my grandfather's assistant at Whitefish Point. However, she was officially appointed—for ten dollars a month mind you—to operate the U.S. Weather Bureau Reporting Station there, which she did for over twenty years," Bertie said proudly.

"I'm afraid your grandmother isn't the only person in your family whose contributions we docents have discounted.

I'm sorry, too, about doubting your German spy story,"
Drew admitted.

"Thank you. I have a few more thoughts on that, but
first—I would ask that when you mention that incident, you
refer to it as my 'account,' rather than my 'story.'"

"Ahh. That's fair. I see what you mean," Drew said as
he nodded in understanding.

"In our family, the adults never played with us as in so
many families. We simply were included in the adults' doings.
This is one of the reasons why I remember as much as I do,"
Bertie explained.

"Anything else? Maybe something more specific to
support your account?" Drew asked with his pen hovering
over his notes.

"Yes. There's this!" Bertie announced as she pointed
her index finger in the air. "I remember many occasions when
my grandmother and Reverend Law would speak at length
with one another, just the two of them, at the kitchen table,"
Bertie revealed as she tapped her finger on the restaurant
table. "My grandmother would say to Reverend Law, seemingly
in jest, that 'God may have His eye on the sparrow that falls,
but the rest of us would be wise to have our eye on the hawks
that circle.'"

"What do you think your grandmother meant by that?"
Drew asked probably thinking that the interview with Bertie
had strayed from the topic at hand.

"Mama Anna had an uneasy feeling about the
Schroeders, almost from the beginning. She expressed this to

Papa C, but he was reluctant to give credence to her 'woman's intuition.' So, what did she do? She deployed a secret agent, in the person of Reverend Law, to conduct, however unwittingly on his part, reconnaissance missions into the other side of the lighthouse. After Reverend Law visited the west side of the house, he would visit the east side where Grandmother would 'debrief' the good Reverend over steaming cups of Söderblandning tea as, conversation by conversation, she built a case against the Schroeders to support the suspicions she, ultimately, shared with her husband and likely this prompted him to act on his own suspicions more quickly."

"I think I'll have to listen much more closely the next time I lead a tour through the kitchen," Drew said.

"I'm sorry, you lost me there," Bertie admitted.

"I meant that if those kitchen walls could talk, I would have a lot more detail to add to my docent notes."

"Ah, I see what you mean now. Going back to the spy matter, the best way to convince you of the truth of my account about the arrest of the German spies is that there was nothing about how I was raised by my lighthouse-keeping grandparents that encouraged or fostered "trading in tragedies" for attention or to augment a story or a memoir. Lighthouse keepers and their families were there to prevent tragedy, not to make capital out of it."

"Nothing I've read so far about lighthouse keepers provided that perspective," Drew said mindfully.

"That's the kind of information you can find in a memoir, by the way." Bertie smirked good-naturedly.

"Noted!" Drew smiled as he gestured in the affirmative with his pencil in the air.

The waiter arrived and placed the check face down on the table, which Bertie deftly slid to her side of the table. "My treat, Drew. I do appreciate your willingness to meet with me."

"Thank you, Miss Bertie. How about I let you have the last word—from the tour that began several hours ago, that is. Your insights are making me think that there may be room in my research for filling in the gaps between the facts to put together an even more credible story."

"Account," prodded Bertie.

"Yes, ma'am. It's been a pleasure to meet you. I wish I didn't have to get going, but..."

"You did offer to let me have the last word," Bertie gently reminded Drew as she leaned in as if to share a confidence. "When people think of lighthouses they think of ships at sea and disasters. For some reason, they believe that each day brings a rescue or a tragedy. If it doesn't, they feel something is wrong. Why? For this to happen people living there would become callused to human suffering. It is the exception—the tragedies and near tragedies—that reminds them why they are there. Between times life must be lived— laughter and pain, boredom, loneliness, shared events and friendships, happiness and tears—all go on. It doesn't matter whether you live in a city or on a lonely jet of land. It doesn't take brains to be miserable. However, it does take brains to live life as fully as possible. See the good in people and applaud. See the bad and forget it. And lend a helping hand when needed."

THE DEDICATION

WHITEFISH POINT LIGHT STATION

SEPTEMBER 14, 1996

On the morning of the dedication, Bertie woke up rather disoriented from a deep sleep. For a brief time, she thought that she might be in her childhood bedroom, but as the morning fog of confusion cleared, she remembered she was a guest in the crew's quarters just across the compound from the lighthouse. She had experienced a sound sleep—untroubled by any dreams. Perhaps, because she had done all her dreaming, or rather daydreaming, during the previous day when she toured the restored rooms of her childhood home.

The dedication service was a nice event with the expected speeches and expressions of gratitude, yet Bertie didn't relish being the center of attention. Nevertheless, after the ceremony, she did find herself enjoying conversations, especially among those who had weekend passes and had been on the tour with her the day before. It was a pleasant surprise to her that a few people wanted her to sign their newly-purchased copies of her memoir. Among them was the young girl who had been reading the ghost stories in the museum shop the day before.

"Hello, Mrs. Carlson," said the girl. "Would you sign my copy of your book, please?"

"I'd be delighted to. I'm actually Mrs. Rollo. Mrs. Carlson was my dear grandmother's name," Bertie said as she took the girl's book in hand.

"You look so much like the dummy in the kitchen!" exclaimed the girl.

"I suppose I do resemble the mannequin," Bertie had to admit as she cringed. She was more comfortable with the flattering comparison of her girlhood photos to the *young* "Bertie" mannequin. Eager to change the subject, Bertie asked, "What was your favorite part about the museum tour?"

"Oh, climbing the tower to the lantern!" The girl replied without hesitation as she pointed to the tower.

"That doesn't surprise me at all. I miss being able to climb those stairs," Bertie said wistfully as she squinted to see the top of the tower. She then looked back at the girl in front of her. "What's your name? I want to sign the book to you."

"Lucy."

"Oh, how lovely," Bertie said with a smile as she wrote. *Lucy, may your childhood be as blessed as mine. Keep reading and asking questions and remember that "truth is stranger than fiction."*

Handing the book back to the girl, Bertie then turned to a middle-aged woman wearing a sweatshirt with the image of a lighthouse on it. "While I was signing the young girl's book, I couldn't help but notice that you had already begun your reading!" Bertie noticed with pleasure.

"I've visited several lighthouses and read even more books about them, but I've never come across a memoir about life at such a place from a child's perspective. I'm eager to keep reading."

"Thank you. I'm glad you've found what you never thought you would! What is your name?"

"Kate, ma'am," she said.

Bertie bent over the book, pausing as she thought about just what she might write. *Kate, you have visited more lighthouses than I have, but I hope that Whitefish Point will be your favorite as it is mine.*

Then yet another individual from the previous day's tour came into view. An older gentleman with a Coast Guard veteran's ball cap stepped up to the table almost like he was reporting for duty. He cleared his throat and said, "I liked how you stood up to that young tour guide about what you remembered about the German spies here. Young people discount what we senior citizens know," he said as he tapped his finger on the top of his cap. "My name's Walt, ma'am."

"Thank you, Walt. I guess we can all remember being young, but not knowing what we didn't yet know!"

Walt chuckled in agreement and then looked at what Bertie had written in his book and seemed pleased as he read to himself. *Walt, thank you for knowing that lighthouse keepers were an important part of our national defense.*

Suddenly, the young boy who Bertie remembered from the tour, appeared around Walt's right leg almost knocking him over by grabbing his pant leg like a Maypole. His mother lunged for the boy saying "Michael!" as she breathlessly apologized to the veteran. Walt smiled kindly as he touched the brim of his cap and stepped away from the table.

"I don't have much time to read," the mother said as she regained her composure and her control of her little boy, "but I'm so intrigued by the subject of your book that I think it'll be a good beach read."

Bertie raised her eyebrows.

"Oh, I'm sorry. That sounds insulting. I mean, I need a book that's not too long, but that also holds my attention. I know that your book will do just that," she apologized as she regained her grip on the belt loop of her son's pants while she reached into her purse and handed him a shiny agate to hold. With her son's attention captured momentarily, she said, "Thank you for signing my book. My name is Mary."

Bertie scribbled as quickly as she could in the mother's book, *Mary, I hope that you will find this a rewarding beach read—set on the shore of beautiful Lake Superior. I also hope that your son will return in the future to Whitefish Point to learn more about the heroic work of lighthouse keepers and their families.*

Drew approached the table after he had waited for all the tourists in line to have a chance to have their books signed. "Good morning, Miss Bertie. I hope that you enjoyed the dedication ceremony this morning."

"Yes, I did, Drew. I was especially moved by the unveiling of the painting of me and my grandfather. That was a truly lovely surprise, but I must admit that I'm relieved that it's all over!"

"That's understandable. I'm so glad that you were on my tour yesterday. And now with the recorded interview and my notes, and your memoir book, which I'd like you to sign, I'll have valuable resources for leading future tours."

"That's quite gratifying, Drew. I'd be honored to sign your book," Bertie said as she quickly rubbed the cramped knuckles of her dominant hand before writing. *Drew, thank you for welcoming people into my childhood home. I entrust you with this important responsibility because you are a thoughtful historian who will enlighten so many tourists about the importance of this site and the souls who lived and served here.*

"I would like to get a photo of you standing in front of the painting of you and your grandfather," Drew requested.

"Of course!" Bertie said as she got up from the table to follow Drew across the compound to where the easel holding the painting was still on display, inside the relative safety of a well-staked tent. Once there, she revisited the memory of the unveiling just a few hours ago. At the time, she was so overcome with emotion at seeing the image that she hadn't fully taken it in that the work was commissioned by the Great Lakes Shipwreck Historical Society. She was too flustered at the time to read the small brass plaque, which was engraved with "*A Whitefish Point Lighthouse Christmas* by artist David Conklin."

Bertie had tried to express her gratitude properly at the ceremony, but she struggled to keep her composure. The artist hadn't created merely an imagined scene from her childhood but had somehow managed to re-create a specific scene deeply embedded in her memory.

"Miss Bertie, I'm sorry to make you wait," Drew said, "but I forgot to get my camera from the locker in the docent lunch room."

"Take your time, Drew. I'll use this opportunity to study the painting more closely," Bertie said to Drew's back as he trotted across the compound.

Bertie took off her glasses to focus on the painting's details. She was captivated by it. There within the frame was her 5-year-old self. It was all as she remembered it. She was trotting alongside her grandfather and with every step the wind buffeted her and the snow drifts nearly swallowed her. She remembered barely managing to keep up with Papa C as he held a lantern in one hand and with the other dragged a freshly-cut Christmas tree behind them. And there, too, were the dogs eagerly leading the procession back to the lighthouse. And there it was all aglow with the light of home and hearth as it had been on so many nights. How had the artist made the scene so evocative of her warmest memories? She mused that the past viewed through the soft-focus filter of nostalgia, like in this painting, was comforting and pleasant, but also brought memories of the past into sharper focus.

The scene in the painting summoned Bertie's recollection of the warmth and the chill of not only the holiday seasons but of their service and sacrifice as a lighthouse-keeping family.

Admittedly, she was disappointed that her brother and particularly her grandmother were not included in this tableau. That realization gave Bertie more than a moment of discomfort in having been singled out since everyone in the family contributed in their own way to the functioning of the light and none more so than her grandmother. Bertie noted that much more attention was paid to explanations of how the lens worked in the lantern than how the multi-faceted role of the lighthouse keeper's wife made everything else work much more smoothly than it would have without her.

Bertie knew that her grandmother had been named as an assistant lighthouse keeper at three different posts over her lifetime. She had told Bertie many stories, but one of the most exciting ones was how she and her grandfather rescued nearly a dozen fishermen from the shipwreck of the *Ora Endress* just a mile from Whitefish Point. When her grandfather received an official commendation from the Lighthouse Board, her grandmother's part in the rescue was completely overlooked. Grandfather, however, always knew Mama Anna's value as his capable unofficial and official assistant.

It was then that Bertie's attention was drawn back to the painting and the light depicted in the image—not the beam from the lantern, but the glow from the windows of the lighthouse keeper's residence. Mama Anna kept that vigil light burning within the house and within Bertie's heart for her whole childhood—indeed for her entire life. Bertie had titled her memoir, *Beneath the Light,* but upon reflection, a better title might have been *Toward the Light*. After all, that's where she and her grandfather were headed in the painted scene— toward the beacon that was her grandmother.

Bertie smiled as she realized that in paying attention to the glow from the house the artist had captured the reality of her life at the light. The beacons were all there in the painting—one for the seafaring folks and one for the family—both beacons incandescent and forever unextinguishable.

ADDENDA

Treasury Department
Light House Establishment
Form 111.—Ed. 5 29 1902 1,500

OATH OF OFFICE

I, Robert Carlson, do solemnly swear that I will support and defend
the Constitution of the United States against all enemies, foreign
and domestic; that I will bear true faith and allegiance to the same;
that I take this obligation freely, without any mental reservation or
purpose of evasion; and that I will well and faithfully discharge the
duties of the office on which I am about to enter; so help me, God.

Robert Carlson

Notarized: 17th day of October A. D. 1903

Name of Office.	Name of Station.	State or Country in which born.	State or Territory from which appointed.
Keeper	White Fish Point	Finland	Michigan

This oath should be taken before a Justice of the Peace, Notary
Public, a Judge of a Court, or any other officer having authority to
administer oaths, but never before a Collector of Customs, as he
has no power to administer oaths in such cases. This oath should
be taken on or before the date of the appointment.

Washington, March 27, 1903

Treasury Department
Office of the Secretary
Division of Appointments
Eleventh District

Mrs. Annie M. Carlson,

Care of the Chairman of the Light House Board.

Madam:—

Your temporary appointment as Acting Assistant Keeper of
the Marquette Light—Station, Michigan, is hereby extended
with compensation at the rate of four hundred and fifty dollars
($450.00) per annum, for the period from December 12 to
December 26, 1902, both dates inclusive.

Respectfully,

(signature illegible)

Secretary

The quote below serves as evidence of planned German spy activities on Lake Superior during World War I.

OPERATION SNOW OWL BY E.J. WALDEN

(excerpt)

This quote is attributed to Albrecht von Graefe as communicated to Hermann Göring, Rudolph Hess, Joseph Goebbles, and Adolph Hitler.

(date unknown)

"There was an attempt during the Great War to install one of our people as an Assistant Keeper of the light at Whitefish Point, which they call the graveyard of Lake Superior. His name was Schroeder, and his task was to disrupt shipping by putting both the light and the fog warning signals out of commission. Unfortunately, the Head Keeper, a fellow named Carlson discovered he had a German spy in his midst and summoned government agents who took Schroeder and his wife off to prison."

Keeper Carlson surely broke with protocol, out of necessity, when he discretely reported Assistant Keeper Schroeder to government agents in July of 1918.

**U.S. LIGHTHOUSE SERVICE INSTRUCTIONS
TO LIGHT-KEEPERS (1902)**

(excerpt)

"When a keeper neglects his duties, it is the imperative duty of each assistant at the station to report the facts without delay, in writing, to the inspector. The reported keeper must be furnished with a copy of the complaints made against him, at least three days before such complaints are forwarded, so that he may, if he sees fit, transmit a statement to the inspector with the report. A keeper reporting an assistant keeper will follow these instructions."

OBITUARY

BERTHA ENDRESS ROLLO
1910-2007

Bertha Matilda Endress Rollo, a long-time member of the Sault Naturalists and the Audubon Society, died at the age of 97 on September 28, 2007. Bertha was a dedicated birder and often spoke at the Chippewa County schools about topics ranging from lighthouse living to ornithology to environmental awareness. She was the granddaughter of the keeper of the Whitefish Point Light Station, and she lived at the lighthouse for her first 21 years.

She married William Rollo, who preceded her in death, and they had one son, Carl.

Bertha graduated from Sault High School with the class of 1928. She briefly attended the University of Michigan but was forced to depart that avenue of education when she contracted rheumatic fever and was bedridden for three years.

She worked as a clerk and cashier in several stores in Sault Ste. Marie, such as Scott's and Montgomery Ward's. During WWII, she worked as an Executive Secretary at Fort Brady in Sault Ste. Marie.

In 1980, she aided in the restoration of the Whitefish Point lighthouse. Bertha provided furniture, pictures, and artwork she had retained when her grandfather retired as lighthouse keeper. She was very instrumental in establishing the lighthouse quarters, offices, and museum.

Upon the occasion of her 90th birthday, longtime friend Paul D. Freedman published a series of her short stories in a book entitled *Beneath the Shining Light.* The stories tell of the adventures of the sailors and her family while residing at Whitefish Point.

Bertha was Grand Marshal of the Paradise Blueberry Festival in 2000. She considered Paradise her second home, and in her book wrote, "What a real paradise! You are all to be envied. You have today what many people would give their all to have."

FAMILY PHOTOS

All images courtesy of the
GREAT LAKES SHIPWRECK
HISTORICAL SOCIETY
Sault Sainte Marie, Michigan

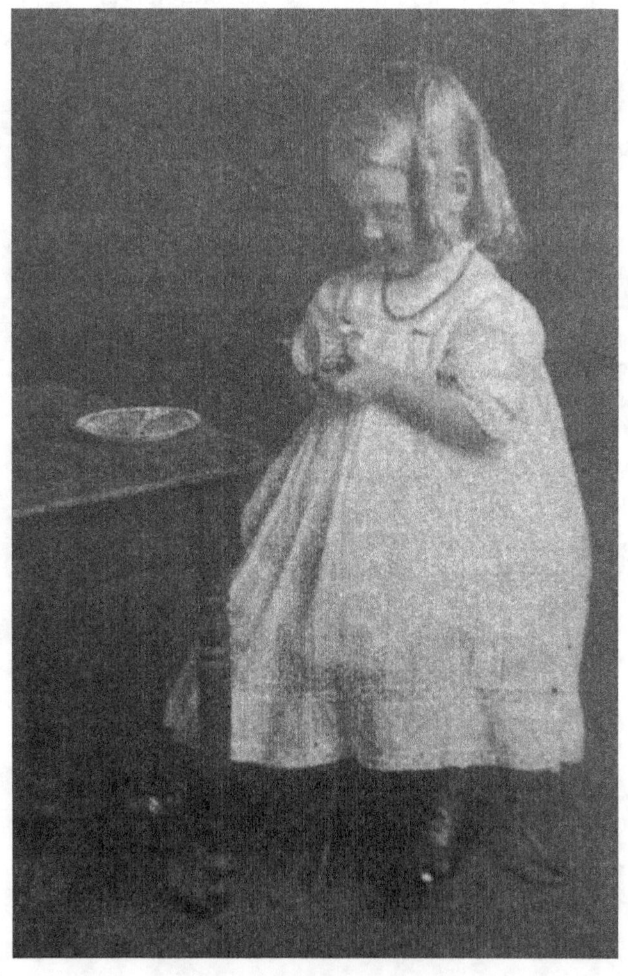

Bertha Endress

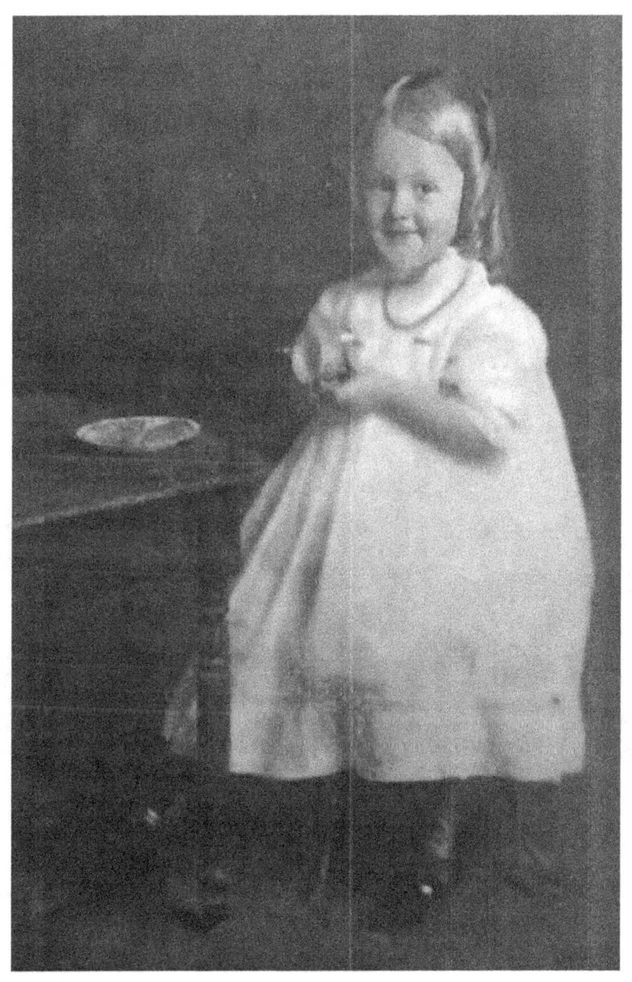

Bertha Endress

Robert Carlson
with granddaughter Bertha Endress

Robert Carlson
with granddaughter Bertha Endress

Robert and Anna Carlson with grandchildren
Bertha & Bobbie Endress

Bertha Endress with Grandfather Robert Carlson
A Whitefish Point Lighthouse Christmas (circa 1920)
[oil on canvas]
Conklin, D.W. (1990)

Whitefish Point Light Station
Paradise, Michigan

ANNA CARLSON'S RECIPE FOR KLADDKAKA OR "MUD CAKE" THE SWEDISH BROWNIE

Ingredients:

- ½ cup all-purpose flour

- ¼ cup unsweetened cocoa powder

- 1 pinch salt

- 2 eggs

- 1 ⅓ cups white sugar

- 1 tablespoon vanilla extract

- ½ cup butter, melted

Directions:

Preheat oven to 300 degrees Fahrenheit (150 degrees C). Lightly grease an 8-inch pie plate.

Sift together flour, cocoa powder, and salt; set aside. Stir eggs into sugar until smooth. Add flour mixture, and stir just until combined. Pour in vanilla extract and butter; stir until well combined. Pour into prepared pie plate.

Bake on lower rack of preheated oven for 35 minutes, or until center has slightly set. Allow cake to cool for 1 hour in pie plate. Serve warm, or refrigerate overnight and serve cold.

ENDNOTES

Epigraph

"There is nothing more frightening or exciting than a blank piece of paper. Frightening because you're on your own, leaving dark tracks across that snowy plain, and exciting because no one knows your destination but yourself, and even you can't say exactly where you'll end up."
(McCammon, p. 227)

Dining Room

"... the Carlson's dining room was a private place for the family of four to gather and enjoy a meal together. Anna Carlson also had to feed the men who came to repair the cribs (or jetties), the submarine bell, or anything that keeper Carlson, or his assistant lighthouse keeper, couldn't fix on their own. In addition to caring for victims of a possible shipwreck, and the occasional guest the family fed, they also took care of the Coast Guard men who came from the Vermilion Station on rescue or training missions, or a group of workers known as 'The Boys' who ate the biggest breakfasts of all, but then they did have to stand in cold water all morning."
("MEALS FOR ALL" Exhibit Sign in the Lighthouse Museum)

"They could smell them coming and had to open the windows wide in the dining room and leave them open until midnight. The family then ate in the kitchen."
("MEALS FOR ALL" Exhibit Sign in the Lighthouse Museum)

"...the stark loneliness of our postings over the years was appalling."
(http://www.bobmackreth.com/Scrapbook/heroine.htm)

Parlor

"... the only radio station they could receive for some time was KDKA from Pittsburgh."
("FURNISHINGS, REGULATIONS & ESPIONAGE" Exhibit Sign in the Lighthouse Museum)

"Mother hasn't spoken to Father
Since she found a hair upon his coat—
And a savory little note—
That some other lady wrote—
Now poor father—he's the goat.
And now it's getting cold around the house!"
(Rollo, p. 41)

Lighthouse Keeper's Office

Letter to the *Department of Commerce Lighthouse Service* Display Case at Lighthouse Museum:
"In keeping the journal two pages are to be used for one month. The events of the day must be written on one line across both pages. If carefully written, one line will be found sufficient..."
("United States Light-House Establishment Instructions to Light-Keepers." Light-House Board, July 1881.
https://media.defense.gov/2020/Sep/11/2002495502/-1/-1/0/1881-USLHS-KEEPER-INSTRUCTIONS.PDF)

Bedroom

"Children of a lightkeeper lived in a world very different from that of children who lived in the cities or even small towns. Every day they were exposed to the realities of nature at Whitefish Point, the beauty of sunrises and sunsets, the drama of seasonal changes, and the harshness of the wind and the power of Lake Superior. Such a relatively isolated life meant that families were very close. Simple little things were important and had a significant impact on children's lives and they developed a special attachment to the world of their lightkeeper parents."
("AN ISOLATED CHILDHOOD" Exhibit Sign in
Lighthouse Museum)

"Of course, a woman can do anything if she sets her mind to it."
(http://www.bobmackreth.com/Scrapbook/heroine.htm)

"The fresh nights of spring, the twinkling lights of passing freighters on warm summer nights, and the cold and deadly gales of November."
("CHILD OF THE LIGHT STATION" Exhibit Sign in
Lighthouse Museum)

"I sat up all night waiting and watching. By the morning, I was in such an anxious state. Then, I realized that I had to milk the cow for the children, but I had never milked the cow and I was afraid of her. She could really kick. I went down to the barn and looked at the cow. She swung her head toward me and made a noise that did nothing to quell my fears and I knew I could never milk her as I had seen your grandfather do. Running into the woodshed, I grabbed the axe, and in desperation began chopping at the wall of the cow's manger. I hacked away at the wall until I had a hole through which I

could put both hands. Then I started to milk into a little tin cup, which I held with one hand, while I milked the cow with the other hand. The cow kicked and I jumped away, but I kept at it for the children's sake."
(http://www.bobmackreth.com/Scrapbook/heroine.htm)

"On the third day I could stand the house no longer. Leaving the little girl with the twins, I put on a hat and coat and went down the shore. You don't know what the Michigan Island shore is, in winter. Unbroken trails through the woods, ice hummocks barring the way, deep gulches of snow into which I stumbled, the bitter, cutting wind from the lake lashing my face; and above all the sight of that white expanse which was holding my husband from me."
(http://www.bobmackreth.com/Scrapbook/heroine.htm)

"Sometimes, when we think we can't endure any longer, it does us good to let go, like that. I think if I had not screamed, I would have lost my mind."
(http://www.bobmackreth.com/Scrapbook/heroine.htm)

"The men finally returned, but not until the eve of the third night. They didn't mean to stay away so long, but the ice had broken up while the men were fishing and the platform of ice that they were on was carried out into the open lake."
(http://www.bobmackreth.com/Scrapbook/heroine.htm)

Locked Door and Long Ago

"Suddenly, we were not let out of the house and a government boat with men I had never seen before appeared. Furniture was taken from the assistant lightkeeper's house and the assistant and his wife were removed in handcuffs. The assistant was sullenly silent, but his wife was screaming and

cursing in English and German. It seems that they had been
sent by the German government to disrupt shipping by putting
the light and fog signal out of commission. I clearly remember
standing at the window upstairs with my grandmother and my
mother, as we watched the couple being taken away."
("FURNISHINGS, REGULATIONS & ESPIONAGE" Exhibit Sign in
Lighthouse Museum)

"1918 was a time of high anti-German sentiment felt
throughout the US, especially against immigrants. Robert
Carlson had two sons, twins who were fighting against the
Germans so he would not have been too keen to have a
German immigrant as an assistant keeper. Also, it was said
that Carlson was not easy to get along with, so there might
have been a conflict between the two lightkeepers for one
reason or another."
(Hanna, notes June 2022)

Lighthouse Tower

"The light was a kerosene mantle light floating on a bed
of mercury. Each night (on every watch) the light had to be
wound up. Weights slipped on a rope that extended from the
light base to within a foot or so off the ground in a special pipe
or tower of its own. It was cranked or wound with a handle and
the weights rose. It was the slow descent of the weights that
caused the lights to turn."
(Rollo, p. 40)

"In 1915, Detroit was the target of a plot to blow up local
manufacturing companies, such as the Detroit Screw
Works, which was manufacturing shrapnel for the Allied
troops. German immigrant and Detroit resident Albert

Kaltschmidt was busy buying dynamite, cutting it into small pieces, painting it black, and tossing it surreptitiously into coal bunkers of vessels in the Detroit River. In May 1915, Kaltschmidt met with several German immigrants in the Kresge Building. He told those assembled that their duty lay in the destruction of munitions destined for the Allies in Europe and asked for their help in blowing up a factory in Detroit, according to Nigel West, author of *The Historical Dictionary of World War I Intelligence*. Kaltschmidt furnished the men with suitcases full of dynamite. Another plan was to send an explosive-laden 'devil car' ingeniously coasting on roller skates into the Port Huron tunnel.

The money Kaltschmidt used to buy the dynamite and to pay the saboteurs came from Count Johann von Bernstorff, the German ambassador in Washington, D.C., and Captain Franz von Papen, who later became Adolf Hitler's vice chancellor.

U.S. authorities had been keeping an eye on the gang for some time. So, it didn't take long for Kaltschmidt and five others to be indicted. Kaltschmidt was charged with conspiring to destroy the Detroit Screw Works and that he conspired to blow up the Grand Trunk tunnel at Port Huron, one of the skates being produced as evidence in the 1917 trial against Kaltschmidt and his co-defendants.

The trial began on December 6, 1917, before federal Judge Arthur J. Tuttle, according to the United States District Court for the Eastern District of Michigan. The trial dominated newspaper coverage. On Dec. 22, 1917, the jury, after deliberating for 14 hours, convicted all but one defendant. Kaltschmidt was sentenced to four years in the U.S. Penitentiary at Leavenworth, Kansas, and fined $20,000. He

served only three years, to the disgust of Judge Tuttle, and was deported soon after."
(https://www.hourdetroit.com/community/the-spies-among-us/)

Little Falls Restaurant

"In our family the adults never played with us two as in so many families. We simply were included in the adults' doings. This is why I remember as much as I do."
(Rollo, p. 41)

"People of the lighthouses are there to prevent tragedy, not to make capital out of it."
(Rollo, p. 12)

"When people think of lighthouses they think of ships at sea and disasters. For some reason, they believe that each day brings one rescue or tragedy. If it doesn't, they feel something is wrong. Why? For this to happen people living there would become callused to human suffering. It is the exception—the tragedies and near tragedies—that reminds them why they are there. Between times life must be lived—laughter and pain, boredom, loneliness, shared events and friendships, laughter and tears—all go on. It doesn't matter whether you live in a city or on a lonely jet of land. It doesn't take brains to be miserable. However, it does take brains to live life as full as possible, see the good in people and applaud; see the bad and forget it, and lend a helping hand when needed."
(Rollo, p. 12)

Addenda

"Oath of Office" document
(Display case in Lighthouse Museum)

Anna Carlson's Appointment Letter document
Interpretive Manual Supplement (for docents at Whitefish
Point), p.25

"There was an attempt during the Great War to install one of
our people as an Assistant Keeper of the light at Whitefish
Point, which they call the graveyard of Lake Superior. His
name was Schroeder, and his task was to disrupt shipping
by putting both the light and the fog warning signals out of
commission. Unfortunately, the Head Keeper, a fellow named
Carlson discovered he had a German spy in his midst and
summoned government agents who took Schroeder and his
wife off to prison."
(Walden, p. 71)

"When a keeper neglects his duties, it is the imperative duty
of each assistant at the station to report the facts without
delay, in writing, to the inspector. The reported keeper must
be furnished with a copy of the complaints made against him,
at least three days before such complaints are forwarded,
so that he may, if he sees fit, transmit a statement to the
inspector with the report. A keeper reporting an assistant
keeper will follow these instructions."
(Interpretive Manual Supplement, p. 25)

Obituary

http://soonats.pbworks.com/w/page/23606430/Sault%20
Naturalists%20We%20Have%20Known

BIBLIOGRAPHY

Cover Image

Conklin, D.W. *A Whitefish Point Lighthouse Christmas*, Circa 1920. 1990.

Artwork commissioned and permission granted for use courtesy of the Great Lakes Shipwreck Historical Society.

Epigraph

McCammon, Robert. *Boy's Life.* Pocket Books (a division of Simon & Schuster Inc.), New York, 1991.

Books

Huttenstine, Jan McAdams. *Remotely Yours: A Historic Journey Into The Whitefish Point Area.* East West Press, Paradise, Michigan, 2010.

Kotzian, John. *Sky Pilot of the Great Lakes: A Biography of the Reverend William H. Law.* Avery Color Studios, Inc., Gwinn, Michigan, 2014.

Majher, Patricia. *Ladies of the Lights: Michigan Women in the U.S. Lighthouse Service.* University of Michigan Press, Ann Arbor, Michigan, 2010.

Planisek, Sandra L. *Reliving Lighthouse Memories: 1930's-1970's.* Great Lakes Lighthouse Keepers Association, Mackinaw City, Michigan, 2004.

Walden, E. J. *Operation Snow Owl.* Booksurge, Eloquent Books, (imprint of Strategic Book Group), Durham, CT, 2010.

Articles

"Sault Naturalists We Have Known." John W. Lehman, editor. Bertha Endress Rollo Obituary. http://soonats.pbworks.com/w/page/23606430/Sault%20 Naturalists%20We%20Have%20Known

"Shedding Light on Michigan's Historic Female Keepers." Promote Michigan Blog, Accessed March 7, 2018. https://promotemichigan/shedding-light-michigan-historic-female-keepers

"The Eastland Disaster Killed More Passengers Than the Titanic and the Lusitania. Why Has It Been Forgotten? Chicago's working poor were expecting a day in luxury. They instead faced a horrific calamity on Lake Michigan." Susan Q. Stranahan. Smithsonian Magazine, October 27, 2014. https://www.smithsonianmag.com/author/susan-q-stranahan/

"The Heroine of Michigan Island," Apostle Island Scrapbook, Accessed April 20. 2024 (originally published in an article by Stella Champney in *The Detroit News,* May 17, 1931). http://www.bobmackreth.com/Scrapbook/heroine.htm

"The Most Precious Cargo for Lighthouses Across America was a Traveling Library." Natalie Zarrelli. Atlas Obscura, February 18, 2016. https://www.atlasobscura.com/articles/the-most-precious-cargo-for-lighthouses-across-america-was-a-traveling-library

"The Sky Pilot of Lighthouses, Pathways of the Heart." Marilyn Turk. July 18, 2014. https://pathwayheart.com/the-sky-pilot-of-lighthouses-2/

"The Spies Among Us." Sheryl James. Hour Detroit, March 27, 2017. https://www.hourdetroit.com/community/the-spies-among-us/

"United States Light-House Establishment Instructions to Light-Keepers." Light-House Board, July 1881. https://media.defense.gov/2020/Sep/11/2002495502/-1/-1/0/1881-USLHS-KEEPER-INSTRUCTIONS.PDF

"USLHE Traveling Library." Michigan Lighthouse Conservancy. September, 22, 2003. www.michiganlights.com/lhlibrary.htm

Memoir

Rollo, Bertha Endress. *Beneath the Shining Light: Memories of the Whitefish Point Light, 1910 – 1931.* Whitefish Eagle News, 2000.

Interpretive Materials

Great Lakes Shipwreck Museum Interpretive Manual Supplement. Great Lakes Shipwreck Historical Society, Sept. 2018.

Interpretive signs posted in each room of the lighthouse keeper's residence at Whitefish Point Light Station by the Great Lakes Shipwreck Historical Society, 1996 (as seen in June of 2022).

An Isolated Childhood [family life]

Child of the Light Station [Bertha Endress Rollo biography, contributions to exhibits]

Furnishings, Regulations & Espionage [entertainment, requirements, eyewitness on espionage]

Keeper of the Light [Robert Carlson's biographical information]

Meals for All [feeding family and visitors]

Tending the Light [lightkeeper responsibilities]

The Busiest Room in the House [kitchen, domestic responsibilities]

The Lightkeeper & His Wife [origins, marriage, and offspring]
Duties, Wages, and Inspections [maintenance of buildings and records]

Docent Notes obtained from Andrew Hanna, June 2022 [personal notes about espionage at Whitefish Point]

Display case at Whitefish Point Lighthouse Exhibit Room

Carlson's Letter to the Department of Commerce (January 5, 1918)

Carlson's "Oath of Office" (October 17, 1903)

Exhibit in the Lifeboat Rescue Station at Whitefish Point

"U.S.L.S.S. Library No.3" mounted on wall

Lighthouse Establishment Library [book selection contents]

Recipe

https://www.allrecipes.com/recipe/75135/swedish-sticky-chocolate-cake-kladdkaka/

Photo Credits

All photos used courtesy of the Great Lakes Shipwreck Historical Society, Sault Ste. Marie, Michigan.

READING GROUP QUESTIONS

1. If you were to write a memoir about your childhood, what would you include as a fond memory or even a pivotal one?

2. How would you characterize your relationship with your grandparents?

3. Bertie had a secret from childhood. Do you have a secret you have been keeping since you were a child? What has the secret represented in your life? Without necessarily revealing what it is, what kind of a toll, if any, has it taken on your life? What do you think should be the statute of limitations for a childhood transgression?

4. Do you find Bertie's recollection credible regarding being an 8-year-old eyewitness to the arrest of the German spies?

5. Does it surprise you that women served as lighthouse keepers?

6. Life as a lighthouse keeper was the very definition of working remotely. What are some of the same aspects and issues related to working remotely in today's world?

7. Did your parent's job(s) affect your life other than that that job helped your parent(s) provide for your family?

8. Can you think of jobs or professions that have an impact on family life something like the families of lighthouse keepers?

9. Have you had to sacrifice your career in service to your spouse's career as Anna Carlson did?

10. Compare and contrast other books about living at a lighthouse that you might have read.

ACKNOWLEDGMENTS

I am appreciative of the following professionals and organizations for their assistance in gaining access to key archival materials for this book: Bruce Lynn, Executive Director and Development Officer of the Great Lakes Shipwreck Museum, Sean Ley, Development Officer of the Great Lakes Shipwreck Historical Society, Docent Andrew Hanna, The Bentley Historical Library (University of Michigan) and The Swedish American Museum of Chicago. I thank my brother-in-law Scott Scholtens for consultation and photo image editing as well as my niece Ilaria Crum for her professional advice regarding citations and permissions.

Wondering whether a writing project might ever come to be, the writer embarks on a long solitary journey. Then, at key moments, she knows that the road ahead cannot be traveled alone, if the destination is ever to be reached. That's when others joined my journey, providing essential help in shepherding me through the twists and turns to arrive at my finished novel.

I am thankful to Roger Crum, my brother, and to Laura Kao, Sandra Planisek, Marcia Russo, and Kevin Williams, prized friends of many years, for their review of several preliminary drafts. Their editorial suggestions ranged from punctuation to plot, but it was their steadfast understanding of the sincerity of my interest in this story and believing that I could write it, for which I am most grateful to them.

Of course, I owe a debt of gratitude to Bertha (Bertie) Endress Rollo. It was her engaging spirit that I discovered between the pages of her memoir about her childhood that has been the guiding light illuminating the path forward in my work.

Also, I was inspired to write this novel because of the generous encouragement of those who read my first novel and had kind things to say about it and even asked me when they could expect to read the next one. It is for you, my essential readers, for whom I took up my pen again.

I am ever grateful to my husband Brian who maintained the ruse that my interest in visiting Whitefish Point was to celebrate our wedding anniversary instead of conducting research and for never doubting that I would eventually write this book. Finally, to my children Michael, Luci, and Vanessa who will one day remember me not only as their mom, but also as a teacher, musician, and writer, *but above all,* their mom.

AUTHOR'S NOTE
INSPIRATION FOR *RETURN TO PARADISE*
JULY 4, 1995

The idea for this novel surfaced from the depths of Lake Superior and turned up in the aisles of the IGA convenience store in Mackinaw City, Michigan on July 4, 1995.

My mother and I had dashed into the small grocery to grab chips and s'more ingredients to contribute to the annual fireworks watch party at a friend's cabin on the shore of Lake Michigan. We were in a hurry so that we wouldn't miss the panoramic view of "The Straits" and the "Big Mac" bridge as the backdrop for the triple fireworks display from St. Ignace, Mackinac Island, and Mackinaw City.

Just as we were putting our holiday snack cache on the conveyor belt, I took notice of a mature man with a solid build all dressed in black with a mass of steely gray rogue waves of hair and a matching beard. He looked like he was straight out of central casting with a Rex Harrison vibe (ala the classic film *The Captain and Mrs. Muir*). I must have thought momentarily that I was in a play because I didn't think the man in black could hear me stage whisper to my mother, "He looks like an old sea captain!" Before my mother could respond, he said, "I *am* a sea captain," as he put his celebratory beverages on the conveyor belt.

He wasted no time in telling us that he was the captain of the expedition that had just the day before brought up the bell from the wreck site of the doomed iron ore freighter, the *Edmund Fitzgerald,* that sank on the night of November

10, 1975. We felt like we were in the presence of a "history maker" as we eagerly shook hands with the man, heartily congratulating him on the success of his mission. That was our story to regale our friends with that evening around the bonfire on the beach. At the time, I thought that the anecdote of the chance encounter was all that there was to be made of the story.

The next day, I read the front-page article in the local paper about the expedition and how the 200-pound bell from the shipwreck at the bottom of Lake Superior would be restored and placed on display at the Whitefish Point Lighthouse Museum. This piqued my interest in visiting Whitefish Point, so my husband and I soon made the trip over the Mackinac Bridge into the Upper Peninsula of Michigan, and to the town of Paradise. There we visited the new home and final resting place of the recovered bell from that storied ship.

We thoroughly enjoyed the museum and, as it turned out, there would be something *else* that would capture my imagination and resonate with me even more than the bell for the next three decades—the fascinating coming together of daily life and historical moment at the lighthouse keeper's residence. With the writing of this novel, I have been on my own mission to discover the novelist deep within me with the help of research, imagination, and keen interest, particularly in historical figures who lived in and indeed shaped the great state of Michigan.

This book is dedicated to my immediate family, my own lighthouse beacon. It is additionally dedicated to all who are, ever have been, and might yet come under the spell of northern Michigan, an incantation I first succumbed to in the company of my father, mother, and brother, all of whom are somewhere here in the pages of this book interwoven in the remembered and re-envisioned lives of Bertie, Bobbie, Mama Anna, and Papa C.